THE COST to Play

Olivia Gaines

Davonshire House Publishing
PO Box 9716
Augusta, GA 30916

This book is a work of fiction. Names, characters, places and incidents are products of the author's vivid imagination or are used fictitiously. Any resemblance to actual events are locales or persons, living or dead, are entirely a coincidence.

Editor: Kathy Riehl, http://www.riehlfaithproductions.com/

Cover: http://koougraphics.net/

Art: Kiara Thomas, http://kiaramotiondesign.com/

Olivia Gaines Make Up and Photograph by Latasla Gardner Photography

ISBN-13: 978-0615948157 (Davonshire House Publishing)

ISBN-10: 0615948154

Printed in the United States of America
1 2 3 4 5 6 7 10 9 8

First Davonshire House Publishing January 2014

DEDICATION

For Kiara, Katsuo is alive.

Be forever vigilant!

Table of Contents

ACKNOWLEDGMENTS

This book was a concerted team effort. I thank each and every one of you for pulling this one together. I have the best team on the planet!

Write On!

Let's begin our story

Chapter 1 -

There are some daybreaks when a body awakens and is ready for the day to commence. It was going to be one of those mornings when a girl felt like she had just stepped into a scene in a Disney movie. The day would begin with that perfect quaint scene in the movie where blue birds fluttered about, flowers bloomed as the pretty girl walked by, and a tune filled the lungs exhibiting how great a girl was feeling. Jayne Wright's mood was just that good as she parked her Chevy Equinox on the street. Today, nothing could dampen her spirit. She began to sing as she made her way to the office. She bobbed her head to the left, swayed her hips to the right, and moved her shoulders to an imaginary beat as she belted out a few notes to an old R & B song. This day could not be more perfect.

"Yo baby! You lucky you got an ass like that. It almost makes up for your singing and dancing," said some man rolling by in a wheelchair on the sidewalk. Jayne gulped as if she had just swallowed a very large bug. The old fart didn't even bother to look back as he continued to roll down the side walk, now singing the same song, but in tune and in key. Even Wheelchair Willie's snarky comment was not going to ruin her day.

Friends often mocked her for giving every person a funny moniker, but it was her thing. It did not matter to Jayne in the least about whether she met with other's expectations of her. It was irrelevant. She was her own person, with her own mind, and her own way of doing things. Her Grandma Pearl often chided her mother, "that's what you get for naming a black Chile Jayne." She liked her name and the person she had grown up to be. Independent, free thinking, and a very talented artist.

Unfortunately her talent on paper did not translate to her abilities with humans. It was even worse when it came to humans of the opposite sex. Her inability to understand and relate to men who wanted her as an arm piece befuddled her mind. It was almost a rude shock to her existence when a man would take her to dinner and make bumbling attempts to have her for dessert. Jayne LaQueeda Wright was not that type of woman. Most days, she wasn't sure what type of woman she was exactly, but it wasn't one that was easy.

Simplicity, however, was how she lived her life. Cawley Public Relations had been her first real job out of college and five years later she was still there. Serving as the lead designer and project manager, her work was on billboards all over Augusta, Georgia. Grandma Pearl even swore she saw an ad in Atlanta as well. It was humorous to her, even though she tried several times to explain it to her Grammy, only a handful of their clients were local. When she returned home one evening with her Clio award, Grandma Pearl whipped out *the bottle* of champagne. Jayne had a hell of a time stopping her Grammy from opening it, considering she had purchased the $3 bottle of Champale when Jayne was still in elementary school. There was no way on God's green earth that she would even partake of that sour bottle of pink vinegar. Instead, Jayne had shown up with an unopened bottle of Dom Perignon. Knowing the frugality of her Grammy, she also brought along a $13 bottle of Freixenet as her back up. Much as she had suspected, Grammy opted for the Freixenet. The bottle of Dom was still in the back of her fridge.

Soon, she promised herself, there would be something to celebrate and someone special to celebrate with. She just had to be patient. Grammy had taught her years ago not to ask God for something and then sit around like a fool worrying about it. "Let go and let God," Grandma Pearl always said, and she learned.

In high school, when the captain of the math club wanted to go all the way and she was not ready, she heeded her Grammy's words and let Ralph go. The adage still buzzed in her head in college, when the chair of the art department said he would give her a "D" in the class if she would not stay for some extracurricular activities. His activities included helping him relieve the tension in his pants. Jayne took it to God in prayer and left it there. After her professor awarded her the "D" for the course, Jayne took her cellphone and classwork to the Dean and played back the professor's request. At the end of the conference between the three of them, the Dean and her professor both agreed she deserved that "A".

She loved her Grammy and her wisdom, but Jayne firmly believed that the good Lord helps those who help themselves. Currently, her vision in self-help included a comic book with a kick ass female superhero and matching costume that would be available in local retail stores. Outside of Bling and Storm, there were very few black female heroines in comic books and she wanted to change that. Change would come after she figured out how to make it all happen. She had the talent, but the confidence to do it was another hairy animal.

In the office, she arrived right on time to her desk, with coffee in hand and still a song in her heart. Today, she was leaving for Columbia, South Carolina to attend an anime conference called Banzaicon. This would be her first conference, or con for short, where she would dress in costume for role play. Jayne had two costumes in her car; one for tonight's ball and one for judging. The one for judging she had made herself and was rather proud of it. Nothing could ruin her morning.

Or at least, so she thought. The second hairy animal she had to contend with weekly, was her pod mate and fellow project leader, Frankie Vale, who was a very flatulent man. It did not matter what he ate, or how much or how little he put away. The man was a walking gas giant of methane. It was not just any gas, but the kind of farts that made your eyes water. One day it was so horrendous, she could have sworn his last rip of odiferous death had removed her eyebrows. It made their work relationship contentious. At one point, Jayne had created an online comic strip of Franc the Farter, who was a crime fighter that used noxious fumes to eradicate his enemy. The strip had become very popular, but Jayne forgot to use a pseudonym. Frankie threatened to sue her if she did not take it down. She threatened to sue him for attempted murder with his fumes. He stopped talking to her, relegating their communications to necessity only.

It did not matter much anymore. She brought a face mask for when they had to work together and often after lunch. She opted to work in the conference room when it was not in use. It was easier for them both and definitely easier on her nose.

She kept her eye on the clock as she closed out her daily work At 11:58. She yelled into the bullpen, “Have a great weekend!” Jayne had sent in her monies for the cost of admission into the con. It was time to play dress up and Jayne was ready to make her mark.

- Chapter 2-

"Professor!" she exclaimed. She stuck her arm high in the air, as if her fingers could touch the ceiling. When she received no response, she called him again stretching her arm even higher, "Professor! Professor!" She was reacting as a small child in need of a bathroom break, wiggling in the seat. Slowly he looked up. First at the clock, then at Mary Elizabeth, whom he privately named *The Riddler*. As he made his way toward her work station, thoughts of freedom floated through his mind. Only three hours left in the work day.

"Yes, Ms. Jones? How goes your project?" He looked over her shoulder at the computer monitor, visually perplexed at what he was seeing. Today's assignment was to draw the *Popliteal Fossa* to include the nerves, but what he saw on screen closely resembled a diagram on how to steal cable. Stern, firm, and with some tempered resolution, he finally responded, "No, Ms. Jones. You are somewhat off in your drawing. Please consult my instructions and begin again." Mary Elizabeth opened her mouth to protest, but the look he gave her provided caution and did not elicit the reaction she wanted. She was aware that the professor wanted no part of her shenanigans.

Dr. Toshi Yamaguchi was one, if not the third best, medical illustrator in the country. In his fifth year as Associate Professor at Georgia Regents University at Augusta, he remained firm and detached, but highly proficient in teaching, writing, and publishing. He was on the fast track to tenure. As a Yale graduate, he had many choices of what he wanted to do and where he wanted to teach. At the age of 30, his real dream was comics. In an ideal world, he would be on staff at Marvel as the lead artist for his own original designs and characters.

In this world, he had broken his wrist in a motorcycle accident, causing some damage to the nerves in his right hand. His parents were broken hearted that he would never be able to hold a scalpel, which was fine by him, but it also limited his ability to hold charcoals, paint brushes, and colored pencils. It wasn't really such a disappointment to Toshi, since he had not truly wanted to be a doctor. In all honesty, he didn't desire to be an academic either. Even though he had the letters, people called him doctor, and his parents were appeased. Somewhat. They now craved grandchildren.

It wasn't about to happen. He liked being single. He loved the freedom to move about and spend his money as he saw fit. The small student loans he had taken out for his education were paid off. The down payment for his house was still in a bank account drawing interest and there was no one to nag him about where he was going this weekend, or why he was spending so much money on frivolous items so he could play dress up.

To Toshi Yamaguchi, fandom was about more than dressing up as your favorite hero. Fandom was a way of life, but also an expensive hobby. His girlfriend Ai, often complains when he departs for conferences for several days, stating that he is going to go broke frolicking with his friends. Often he would joke with her about fandom, coming back with a quick retort, "it costs to play with the big boys."

Ai reminds him weekly that it costs to play with a grown woman as well. In his mind, Ai was an unwanted expense and a distraction. The sex was mediocre, leaving her place in his space, dwindling in value. Toshi checked the clock again. It was almost time. "Do not forget your homework assignments which are due on Tuesday. Remember the upper and lower lateral and medial borders of the *Popliteal Fossa* are due in eAssignment and hard copy in color when you walk in the door."

Mary Elizabeth's hand flew up again, but Toshi ignored her. Many of his student surveys would come back, with comments that he appeared to be unfeeling. That was untrue. He felt everything. Right now, the main emotion coursing through his body was disdain. Mary Elizabeth had a crush on him and used any means she could find to get his attention. He'd had it and he wanted her out the door. It was time for the weekend and he had a conference to get to as well as a Samurai suit to get packed. "Have a great weekend," he told the students as they walked out the door. He looked at Mary Elizabeth. "If you are thinking about how to complete the assignment, then you are thinking too much. Draw, draw, and draw some more." A quick closing of his MacBook and he was out the door. He popped his head into his office and waved good bye to the office assistant, Ms. Banks, before heading to the parking garage.

Before he reached the car, he received a call from Ai. "Toshi, we need to talk." Again, another distraction. He responded in a quick clipped tone, "Fine. Meet me at 5 at the Soy Noodle House on Broad Street." He did not give her a chance to respond. He hung up and hurried home. Everything was ready to go, he just needed to load the car. He was on his way to Columbia, South Carolina for Banzaicon. This was the first con where he was entering the costume competition. The larger cons are intimidating to some people and even more so to Toshi as an academic, but at this con he was ready to take on the challenge. He had never been to a smaller conference and was excited to debut his new Silver Samurai costume.

In his heart, at each conference he attended, he hoped to find a friend, or someone who understood him. Someone who would appreciate the craftsmanship of his homemade suit. He knew that Ai, was never going to be that person.

Toshi arrived at the Soy Noodle House at 4:50 and picked a table in the corner close the window, but also close to the door. In his mind, this conversation was going to be short. Ai arrived five minutes later, still wearing her work clothing and lab coat. At five foot seven with shiny black hair, a perfect set of teeth and a warm smile, Toshi was filled with regret that he could not find it in himself to love her the way she deserved to be loved. Ai Tomita was a great dentist who was loved by all of her patients, anyone who came into contact with her, and others who thrived just being in her light. Yet for Toshi, he felt dim whenever he was with her; further playing into the irony of their relationship. It was more troubling to him that her name meant "love". For him, he could only get as far as a cordial fondness for her. She whined incessantly about him being cold and unfeeling, but he did not know how to express to her that he had strong feelings about almost everything else. As she walked up to the door, his heart should have skipped a beat to see her approaching, instead what he felt bordered on apathy.

He rose to greet Ai, helping her with her chair, before reseating himself. He had already ordered a pot of hot tea. She poured him a fresh cup and one for herself. There it was. That sigh. It was a sound that curled his toes inside his shoes. A sound of disappointment and angst in one exhalation, followed by a cluck of her tongue and a nibble on her bottom lip. Then came the condescending words that grabbed a man by his balls and shook him to his core. The private nickname he had given her was *Ball Buster*. "Toshi, I was hoping that this weekend you would change your mind about the *play thing* in Columbia and go with me to Atlanta, to be with our friends."

Ai's condescending attitude had rubbed him the wrong way, especially the way she said *play thing*. He wondered how much it would hurt her feelings if she knew he felt pretty much the same about her role in his life. At this point, Toshi had already resigned himself to be free, which made him fail to speak his mind. "I was hoping you would change your mind and come with me."

Ai sipped at her tea, "I am sorry, but I must say this. You are going to have to decide Toshi. Either we will have a life together, or you can continue to play your dress up superhero games."

"Fine," he said, as he returned his tea cup to its saucer

and rose to leave.

She was shocked. “So does this mean you are coming to Atlanta with me?” He rested his hand upon her shoulder, giving her a saddened look.

“No, it means that I am headed to Columbia to do my *play thing.*”

Ai’s mouth was moving but no words were coming out. Toshi leaned forward, taking her chin into his hand, while pushing the flailing jaws together. “Let me help you Ai. It means that I am not choosing you.”

She stared at him with lips now taut. He made an attempt to soften the blow. “I like you enough to let you go so that you can be with someone else, who can be all the things you want and need in a husband.” He lowered his head and placed a light kiss upon her cheek. He was going to be late to the ball if he didn’t get a move on.

Before Ai could say anything to him, he stood in front of the window and took out his cell phone. She watched his practiced fingers move across the screen. She knew he had turned it off for the weekend. It was one of the many traits that bugged her to no end about Toshi, but indecisiveness was not one of them. Once he made up his mind that was the end.

Toshi Yamaguchi had just dumped her. When he had to make the choice between dressing up as a crime fighting superhero and drawing comics, or being with her, he opted to be the super hero. In her mind, his actions were villainous. He had just made a down payment on a new enemy and she was not going to let this go lightly. There would be no way to explain to her parents how she had managed to run off another potential husband.

Chapter 3

At 4:00 pm on Friday afternoon, Toshi dressed as Gambit from the X-Men and headed downstairs to the hotel lobby to mix and mingle with the other conference attendees. Many con junkies came early to meet the prettiest ladies and maybe score a conference hook up. This had only happened twice for him, but he was single again, so his mind was open to the possibilities. Slipping into the black seamless pants, and picking up a deck of cards, he held up an ace of spades to any woman who caught his eye. Thus far, there had been only two. So many of these attendees were very young and if any reminded him of a student, he shied away.

Vendors had set up earlier in the afternoon. At such a small con, there weren't many writers, artists, or designers present, but Toshi had been tapped to teach two of the classes on Saturday. One in the morning and the other in the afternoon. He was looking forward to it. As he passed by the vendor room, he nearly kept walking but was halted by a vision of delightfulness bent over into a bin of buttons and tchotchkes. In his mind, he hoped it was a woman. The purple Lycra pants, black hair, and a glimpse at side boob said female. It would be most uncomfortable for him if she were not. Feeling confident, he leaned down and whispered close to her ear, "that has to be the most perfect ass I have ever seen."

The princess with the perfect posterior turned slowly, raised her body to full height, and faced Toshi with a look of disgust, "you do realize you said that out loud, right?"

The directness of her tone made Toshi step back. He was also surprised to see that she was a black woman, with a whole lot of attitude. The heels she wore gave her an additional few inches in height, but he imagined her in stocking feet to stand only at five feet maybe four inches. She had full lips and deep, wide set brown eyes that looked like pools of liquid milk chocolate. She had a gap in her teeth and the cutest nose he had ever seen on any woman. Initially, he had thought the hair to be a wig, but as he stared at her, it did not take long to understand it was actually her hair.

"I meant to say it loud enough for you to hear me," he added with a cockiness that was unlike him. Being dressed as Gambit, he felt stronger, more powerful, and far more daring than he should. "At least I didn't ask you to sit it in my lap." He stood with his legs shoulder width apart, his arms folded across his midriff, calling her out. By making such a bold move, Toshi also noticed that his heart rate had increased.

Toshi thought she looked extremely hot dressed as Bling, and much like the comic book character, attitude and angst radiated from her. Jayne was staring at the costumed man, but it was unclear if behind the mask he was Japanese or Chinese. What was evident was the man was arrogant and thought she was an easy mark. She moved closer to him, bringing a smaller smile to his face as she extended her index finger, wiggling it, beckoning him to come closer. "I like the costume Gambit and I like how you decided to take a gamble, but I have to let you know something very important." She paused to drive home the words she was going to hit him with, "but…."

Toshi leaned closer to hear what she had to say. He placed his hand upon his chest in mock chivalry, but it was really an effort to quell the rapid beating of his heart. She smiled as she delivered the words, "you are an asshole."

He reacted as if he had been slapped. She pushed him to the side and walked passed him heading into the conference registration area. He watched her sashay away with more than a casual interest. The initial assessment had not changed. That was still the most perfect ass he had ever seen in his life, but the woman who owned it, was a handful. He found himself with a very wide grin that harbored a very playful thought. *That ass was a perfect handful as well.*

Toshi felt stimulated by her. Her words had hurt his feelings. That was something that had never happened before and he did not like the idea of her thinking of him as an asshole. He called after her. "There you go again, just walking away from the team."

The lady stopped dead in her tracks. Giving just enough of a turn. "I was never truly a part of the team."

She walked away. The faint scent of her perfume still lingered in the air. It was mixed with whatever she used on her hair. Toshi's body reacted. Emotions flooded through him and confusion was knocking at the chunks of blockades that had grown into his cerebral cortex. He had slept with a black woman before, actually, all races of women, but never really considered it anything other than a physical release. Yet that creamy skinned vixen, moved him. For the first time in several years, he felt something stirring him up.

This was going to be a great weekend.

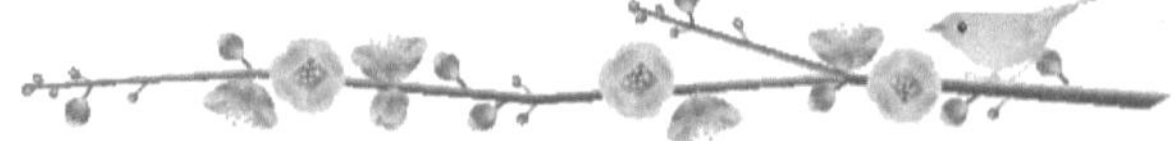

Jayne was an artist and a very good one, but there were two things Jayne was not; easy and easy going. Comic books and painting were her first love, cosplaying was her second, with costume designing coming in a close third. Men were something she had little time for, although her body frequently reminded her of the important role they played in the life of a woman. More so if she planned to procreate. However, children were nowhere on her list of things to get done in her lifetime. Her experience with men had been limited, with only one serious sexual partner to her credit, whom she seldom spoke of nor had many fond memories. Alex had been the first man she been intimate with. Time was moving along at such a clip, that there was little time left to worry about the insignificance of a warm body next to her in bed. Although most conferences served as hookups for the lonely and disenfranchised, for her, this conference was her opportunity to display her newest anime outfit, make a few contacts, and hopefully have a remote chance of winning a prize.

The insulting man in the vendor shop had been just another testosterone filled moron who wanted to get into her pants before getting into her head. Her eyes grew wide at the mere thought of the stories she could tell about the misunderstandings from men who wanted to be a part of her world, but really did not understand what she was trying to accomplish. Jayne wanted to be a costume designer and design an original comic book character.

She lived art. She drank art. In her free time, she breathed comics and she knew this year was going to be her swan song. This year she was going to debut her comic book even if she had to self-publish it on Kindle or Blurb. The work was good. The script was even better. The art work was high caliber, but it was lacking something. She could not put her finger on it, but there was still some time to figure out the defunct.

At 28 years old, Jayne had scored her job with Cawley Public Relations after an internship her senior year in art school. She had not planned to stay with the company for five years, but it was a good fit. Moving back home had not been an easy decision, but her Grammy was getting up in age and the break up with Alex had nearly cost her the small amount of sanity that was left over after sketching and scribbling fictional characters. Occasionally, she would make it to a con and get to dress up as one of her favorite characters as well.

Cosplaying to her was a step beyond *LARPing* and far more fun. Cosplay was a great way for costume designers to get together and show off their craft. The conferences allowed other comic book, fantasy, and science fiction lovers to get together and play games. To her, there was a big difference between cosplaying and LARPing. LARPing is live action role-playing, where the characters actually create scenarios and reenact scenes. That was just a bit too geeky for Jayne's taste. However, getting a chance to don a costume and become the character, changed the way she felt about herself. She loved how the costumes made her feel. In costume, she was powerful and pretty.

Commanding. Admired. Loved.

None of the things she exhibited in real life. In real life, she was a petite weird black woman, with crazy hair, a gap in her teeth and dreams that men did not understand. Even her mother didn't understand her. She felt at times that her friends were humoring her when they listened to her stories. Eventually, she had stopped sharing her ideas. None of what she said was coming to fruition, so it was all just a pipe dream. Or so it had been. This weekend, she was going to change her fate. Winning this costume contest was going to change her storyline. This was going to move her dream forward.

Something made her come to a stop. Besides the several people wanting to take photos with her, she felt eyes boring into her back. Slowly she turned around and spotted the Gambit dude still watching her. Camera flashes were going off as she posed with a few children, two men, and the last one she took, she posed in a fighting stance. The shock she felt when she realized she was posing with Gambit was almost too much. The charge between the two of them was palpable.

A small crowd began to gather as Gambit slid into another pose. Not to be outdone, she altered her stance to a second pose matching him. The crowd began to chant as Gambit pulled playing cards from his pockets and sent them flying into crowd. In a flash, he grabbed her by the hand and pulled her close, segueing into a third pose that caused the crowd to go mad. He held her close with his hands in the small of her back. She could feel the power of his thighs pressing against her own while the male part of him pressed to her delicate part as he hoisted her thigh to ensure she felt his enthusiasm. The kids were all smiling. The flashes from the cameras had nearly blinded her, but she got a grip on herself. Without making a scene, Jayne pulled away, bowed to the audience, and kowtowed to Gambit, making eye contact with him while mouthing the words, “asshole.”

She rounded the corner with Toshi on her heels, but the throng of people closed in on him wanting more pictures. He would not be able to get to her in time and he felt antsy, charged up, excited and ready for.......whatever. He wasn’t sure. Toshi knew that whatever it was, it included that woman.

Jayne rounded the corner, out of breath and full of conflicted emotions. When Gambit took her hand, the sparks that flew up her arm were electric. The man was a pig to even pull her in close like that, so she could feel the pure maleness of his body. It was offensive! Yet, she had never experienced such an intense feeling with anyone.

Chapter 4-

The light from the ceiling was cascading down on the dais, illuminating the strong facial features of the instructor. Jayne watched with some amusement as she eyed his strong jawline, high cheek bones, and Asian eyes. His irises were dark, giving him an aura of mystery, intrigue, and a hint of something she could not mash her finger into. Something felt familiar about him, but his skill set with shadowing was amazing. Each stroke of his wrist sparked her imagination as he tinted the panels of each comic book cell, demonstrating how to darken areas of the body to simulate motion. It was uncertain if the attraction she was feeling derived from his talent or the confidence which radiated from his role as an instructor. Either way, Dr. Toshi Yamaguchi was sexy as hell to her.

She had never dated an Asian man, nor had any interest in doing so until now, but this man was giving her second thoughts. First that Gambit dude, now him. She thought back to her philosophy professor, who found Freudian meaning in every occurrence. She had met two very different Asian men in two days. One she found completely repulsive. The other, she found fascinating. The soft confident way in which he delivered the two hour block of instruction was followed along with a trancelike state of conference goers. Jayne found herself hypnotized by his words and enlightened with his instruction.

Banzaicon was only the fourth conference that Jayne had attended in her life. Outside of her run-in with that Gambit guy, she was enjoying herself immensely. After the check in on Friday night, she noticed two new classes had been added to the schedule. *Shadowing Techniques for Comics*, and *Creating Original Characters*. She jumped at the chance to take the courses. Thus far she had not been disappointed. The instructor was absolutely phenomenal as he used his tablet to sketch out designs, while having the audience follow along. Jayne was even more impressed that he left the make shift stage to walk through the room to check the progress of each of the attendee's work before he moved on to the next technique. At some instance during the instruction, it was twice as impressive that Dr. Yamaguchi laid eyes on every single drawing in the room, providing quasi one on one with every attendee in the session. This was doubly impressive, considering it was standing room only. The younger fans were eating it up, when he looked at their pages, giving canned responses of "good, a little darker here," or "great job." Jayne even found she puffed up a bit when he glanced at her work, stating "good eye for detail." Now she felt foolish because he smelled good too. She was fighting back the urge to get all goofy like many of the women on the front row were.

In the final steps of the drawing, Dr. Yamaguchi employed an old technique of using time lapse to dictate shadow. "Start your shadowing technique at noon. To simulate running, shift the shadow to two o'clock, then three in the next frame." Jayne had never considered such a thing, but when he demonstrated his idea in three panels, the whole room said, "ahhh." Before long, the two hours were up. Dr. Yamaguchi thanked everyone for coming.

The young women flocked to the instructor as Jayne sat, still sketching out an idea that had come to mind based on his last words. No other course had been planned in this room until after lunch, so she continued to work, drafting through her ideas. She was listening, but not listening. As the instructor escorted the women to the door, his deep voice reminded her of the bad guy in the Karate movies who always came into the whore house and drank up all the Sake. He told the young ladies, "I must leave now to grab a bite to eat, before the next session. Excuse me." She found herself smiling as she mimicked, "ah, yes, Mr. Woo, so glad to have you in our fine establishment." She let out a pretend courtesan giggle like she had heard the Asian women do in the movies.

One of the young ladies asked him to join her, but he declined, saying he had already committed to having lunch with a friend. Jayne heard that part from his practiced lines and just imagined his new friend as some dim-witted ingénue in a Sailor Moon costume. Dr. Yamaguchi's deep voice was rich with southern undertones and dripping with the practiced ease of a very expensive education. The ladies sounded disappointed, but he turned to Jayne asking, "Are we ready my friend? I am starving."

Jayne looked over her shoulder to see who he was talking to and spying no one else in the room, she quickly realized it was her. The look on his face was asking for a rescue which made her gather her things and say, "sure thing ole pal. Ready when you are."

He opened the outer door for her and led the way to the hotel restaurant. "I only have an hour or so before the next session, so I hope you don't mind eating here and..." he paused, cutting her a slide glance. "...you do know I heard you back there?"

She gulped, lowering her head in shame at the racial stereotype she had projected, mumbling an apology. She would make it up to him over lunch. Jayne had not realized how hungry she had been until she smelled the food. The hotel restaurant did not seem like a good idea, but most of the conference attendees were headed out for pizza or sandwiches, which left the lobby seating open. Toshi pulled out a chair for her then went to the bar to grab a couple of menus.

What are you doing here with him? Wild thoughts ran through her mind that it was going to be the prickliest lunch ever, but to her surprise it was not. The conversation was light after he thanked her for coming to his rescue. His voice remained steady as he said, "I love to attend cons, but I am uncertain if many of the attendees are even old enough to drink, so I err on the side of caution."

"You seem to have a great number of groupies for an artist."

He smiled as he raised his hand for the waiter to come over. "Art is sexy. I am an artist." He arched an eyebrow indicating that she needed to deduct the final formula.

"You are a sexy artist," she said in a flat voice. It more of a question that a logical deduction.

"Really, you think so? I thank you." He let out a chuckle before adding, "have you decided what you would like?"

Jayne looked at the menu and decided on a Chicken

Caesar Salad, as she watched him over the rim of her glasses. He ordered a pot of tea. Since she had been insulting before, she felt she needed him to understand that she was not ignorant of his culture. When the tea arrived, she stood and kowtowed to him while filling his tea cup. She poured a bit for herself then took a seat. He watched her with some interest, but his facial expressions were indecipherable.

As the food arrived, he ate rice with chopped vegetables and Sautéed Chicken, as he reviewed notes and sketches. It felt peculiar to sit here like this with him, sharing a meal, yet it was perfectly comfortable. They were sharing a space, but not sharing each other. He had not asked her name and she had not volunteered to provide him with it.

She looked up from her salad and found him staring at her. "What?" she asked.

"There is something about you that speaks to me," he said as he cut into the last chunk of chicken.

Jayne wasn't sure if it was a pick up line or another smart ass comment. "Thank you," was all she could muster. He sat there waiting for her to say something.

"What?"

"I don't know," he said as he shrugged his shoulders. "There is something about you. Your qi is calling to me." His heart rate had picked up again. This was an uncommon reaction for him around a woman. Although he had been with a few black women before, she *felt* different. It unsettled him.

"I thought Chi was a Chinese term," she said while continuing to eat her meal but looked at her watch.

"Qi, or, chi and even Xi, are terms that are in several languages. All meaning life force. I don't know what it is about you...." His words trailed off as he eyed the check.

There was a quick demonstration on Kimono making in one of the break out rooms that she wanted to see before going to his next session on creating original characters. She picked up her purse, grabbed a twenty from her wallet, and laid it on the table. "Well, today is not the day for you to figure it out." She bowed again and told him to take care as she headed down the hall to the demonstration.

There was something about him as well that made her feel off kilter. She didn't like it...not one bit. Playing with a man like that always came at a price and she was unwilling to pay the toll.

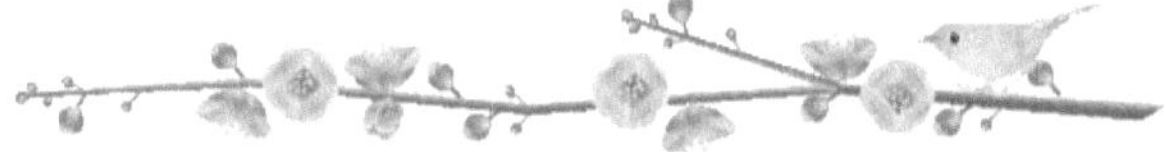

The afternoon class was equally phenomenal as Dr. Yamaguchi showed the attendees how to use a favorite personal photo as a template to create an original character. The sound of pencils against sketch pads making strokes and shading, radiated throughout the crowded room. As he had earlier in the morning, Toshi milled through the throng of sketchers, who had laid out on the floor, leaned against the walls, and occupied every chair, as they presented their work to him at the midway point. The latter portion of the session, he taught his makeshift students the importance of drawing muscles, muscle tone, and muscle sinew. Jayne was amazed at how much better her earlier sketch looked after applying these newly learned techniques. She found herself staring at him absently.

As if he felt her eyes upon him, Toshi turned catching her unaware, meeting her gaze. His heart beat sped up when their eyes connected. *What was it about this woman?* He quickly shifted his focus so his body would not betray him. At the end of the session, he was flocked by conference goers with a ton of questions. He looked for her, but she had disappeared.

Jayne was uncomfortable with the intensity of the connection she was feeling with the good doctor. Maybe she was responding to his artistic ability. It was a foolhardy assessment. The woman in her was responding to the man in him. She shook it off and headed to her room to change for the Cosplay event at 6 pm.

Jayne was planning to debut her costume as Pirotess, from *Record of Lodoss War*. Uncertainty was ringing through her mind as she wondered if anyone would know who she was or even *get* the character. It was all she had, so she was going to go with it. Earlier she felt a great deal of confidence. Now she was uncertain. Three weeks had been spent creating the costume, ensuring that every minute detail had been covered, even working her body out extra hard. Threads, stitches, and fabric choice were all very important when designing a costume. Even more important was the flow of material when on the body. It was these details that she hoped would give her a placing in the show. She checked her hair, her makeup, and adjusted the girls in the suit.

The time had flown by and it was time to head downstairs.

Entering the elevator, there were several Lolita's, *Dragon Ball Z* characters along with other sub characters from *Sailor Moon.* The show stopper was the *Silver Samurai* in the lobby. The detail of the costume was bordering on amazing as many walked up to him to touch the leather and fabricated pieces. As Jayne walked by him, he drew his sword, placing it in front of her to block her path. She could not see his face but immediately knew it was the jerk from last night who was dressed as Gambit. A quick shove with her hand and she pushed the sword aside and made her way to the judging stage. The costumes had been judged earlier yesterday, so tonight was just a formality.

One by one the characters filed on stage, role-playing in the costumes and showing off their handy work. The Silver Samurai was a skilled martial artist and swordsman. The audience oohed and ahhed as he maneuvered from posing to performing high flying kicks for two and a half minutes. Jayne felt sexy as Pirotess when she climbed on stage. She posed and showed a bit of skin as she sauntered across the platform.

The waiting was brief since many of the costumes had already been judged. Three of the *Dragon Ball Z* characters had placed with honorable mentions. An online comic series had received third place for one of the characters, which received great audience response. Jayne was excited when she was awarded second place. The Silver Samurai received first place. Standing close to him, she understood why. He looked really good in the costume with his muscles bulging through the taut leather, his shiny black hair hanging from under the helmet, and those intense eyes gazing through the eye slots.

The winners were all lined up on stage for a quick photo op and then the group began to disperse. The samurai touched her arm beckoning her to follow him. She trailed him into a corner and he removed his helmet. Jayne's eyes were wide when she realized Gambit, the Silver Samurai, and Dr. Toshi Yamaguchi were the same person!

Toshi asked her, "What are your plans for tonight?"

"I plan to go to the party and have a drink or two," she told him waiting to see if he would ask her to dinner.

"I am heading to my room." He turned and began to walk away. "Come with me." It was said with such matter-of-factness that Jayne stood there blinking after him. He looked back to see why she was not walking along with him. He extended to her his hand in a quieter request.

"What am I going to do in your room?"

Toshi's eyebrows went up, "I was hoping…me."

She couldn't believe it. "You know you said that out loud?"

Toshi moved closer to her. "Would it have more impact if I whispered it instead?"

Jayne was disgusted with him. All of her admiration for his talent had flown out the window. She tried to step around him, but he extended his hand to stop her. "There is something about you that stirs my blood. I want to be with you. I am being honest by telling you what I want."

"It seems like you would want to know my name first, Professor. And you know what…?" she paused with her hand on her hip. "I was wrong about you. You are not an asshole, you are a *fucking* asshole."

Toshi moved so quickly Jayne was startled. He stood toe to toe with her. His breath, caressing her cheek as he leaned into her ear. "Pirotess, Bling, or whatever you want to be called, you are amazing. You are a talented artist and you are making me crazy, but I understand. There have been so many men that have lied to you. The truth is hard for you to accept."

"I can accept the truth just fine. I don't accept you wanting to use me as a personal plaything."

He lowered his voice to a whisper, using a sensual and sultry tone. "I don't plan to use you. I plan to give you hours of pleasure." He said it in such a way, that her body said yes, but her mouth said, "thanks, but no."

She stepped around him and headed for the elevator. The idea of going to the party no longer seemed fun. In the morning she would check out and head home. That jerk off had just ruined her night. She hoped he spent the rest of the night doing just that as well.

Unfortunately, her wish for him would probably not come true. A flock of women surrounded him. Some were subtle, while others were direct, using their bodies to gain his attention. She looked back at him once more and was surprised to see his attention was not on the women, but instead on her. Jayne's brain was screaming at her to keep moving, but her body was crying, begging her to go back. She shook her head at him, then moved on to the elevator.

Chapter 5

On a cool and crisp Saturday morning in November, Jayne headed downtown to sketch by the Savannah River. One of the things she truly loved about Augusta was the feel of the city. Although it was the second largest city in Georgia, it was still run like a small town. The quaint feel of the downtown shops and friendliness of the shop owners, made each person feel as if they belonged. The thing she hated about Augusta was the separation. It was a guild town, and *like* hung out with *like*. Nurses who worked at a downtown hospital did not socialize with nurses who worked at an East side hospital. Soldiers hung out with other soldiers, factory workers spent time with other people they worked with, and neighborhoods were divided by income and employers. It made it difficult to make friends.

The Savannah River snaked through the outskirts of the city and served as a dividing line between Georgia and South Carolina. On the Georgia side of the river was a walk path and two concert venues. The larger, was named after a local opera singer who made good and was called the Jessye Norman Amphitheater. The second was a smaller stage for Sunday night jazz in the summers provided by Garden City Jazz. In November, it was just another place for a lonely woman to feel even lonelier.

Jayne's thoughts traveled back to the weekend in Columbia at the con. Dr. Yamaguchi, that asshole, still made her angry whenever she thought about him. The nerve of that man, telling her that men had been lying to her about what they wanted and that he was being honest. The one thing that truly crossed her mind and haunted her dreams were his words. "*I plan to give you hours of pleasure.*" If he was being honest about that, maybe she should have taken him up on it. Yet, reality told her, she could not make a silk purse from a sow's ear. That man was the whole pig.

She gaze down at her pad, liking what she had drawn thus far. Next month was the Atlanta Comic Convention, which had some really good guest speakers. She was planning to attend dressed as Misty Knight, a former X-Men character that Jayne identified with. She was a self-sufficient black woman. Misty was bionically enhanced and a martial arts expert that was never over sexualized in the comics. Even better, she never waited for any man to come and rescue her.

There were noises coming down the side walk and several young men were headed her way. Misty may not need anyone to rescue her, but Jayne knew if she stayed here, a group of young men and a woman alone was just too easy to pass up. She grabbed her pad and made haste for the stairs. She did not stop or look back until she had gotten into her car and locked the doors. Her stomach had started to grumble a bit after the light breakfast of yogurt and granola. Before food, she needed to stop at Joann's and look at some fabric.

Inside the craft store, she had gotten distracted by trimming for her costume. *Step away from the rabbit hole Alice*! She cautioned herself while her empty stomach reminded her of a need for sustenance. Fabric. She came to look for fabric. The selection of material for costumes was not very great here and she was upset that there was no leather. Only pleather and faux leather looking material. The better materials were on the bottom shelf as she initially squatted to view the bolts, extracting one to get a closer gaze.

She heard the voice and did not even need to turn around to know who it was. "I think this is more than a coincidence, or there are two women in this world with a perfect ass like that."

Jayne turned to see Dr. Yamaguchi standing behind her. She was beginning to feel like a parrot. "You do realize you said that out loud right? Do you have any filters?"

He laughed a hearty deep chested laugh, mainly because he was so happy to see her again. "Evidently, when it comes to you, I must not."

She found herself smiling as he extended his hand for a shake. "I am Toshi Yamaguchi."

This was better. She accepted his hand shake. "Jayne Wright." Her stomach growled loudly and he chuckled at the sound of her blatant need for food.

"Jayne Wright. May I have the pleasure of taking you to lunch?"

Her stomach growled again and she looked down at it. "Hush up Timmy. I am going to feed you." Toshi's brows went up.

"I am sorry. Are you married, taken, or expecting?"

Jayne parroted herself once more. "Filters ...Toshi Yamaguchi...filters. No I am not pregnant, married, or taken. Timmy is my hunger monster and he needs food."

The look of relief on Toshi's face was surprising to

Jayne. For that reason, she accepted his lunch invitation.

"The Chop House is across the street," he told her. He made his way toward the check-out counter with a Stone Styler Stud Setting Starter Kit and stud refills. Jayne eyed his items with some interest. "They are for a vest that I am working on," he told her as he presented his teacher discount card at the register.

Jayne made a mental note. Dr. Toshi Yamaguchi was a teacher. This information she stored in her mind as she went to her car and followed behind his Mazda through the Kroger parking lot so they could reach the traffic light. She was actually going to lunch with this man. *What are you doing Jayne?*

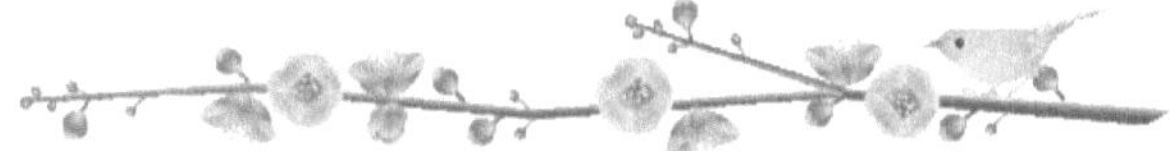

"Bring your sketch pad," Toshi told her as she climbed out of the car. *How did he know she had one with her?* He followed behind her for a moment. She knew he was watching her ass, but he suddenly stopped short and checked his pockets. "Wait! I forgot my tea."

The liquid silver colored Mazda 3, looked exactly like something he would drive. It only took him a minute to retrieve the tea and place it in his left pocket. In his right hand he held a sketch pad and a tin of colored pencils. The walk would have been in silence if Timmy hadn't intruded into the dead air between them. Who knew that grumblings from a hungry stomach can serve as an ice breaker between two people. It made the possibility of spending some time with him seem, well, almost pleasurable. Despite what his mouth would fail to hold back, Jayne was pleased that Toshi was a gentleman by opening the door for her.

Inside the restaurant Toshi quipped, "good. The fire place is going. Do you mind if we sit in front of it?"

"Fine by me." She didn't care if they sat on the floor. All she wanted was food. Lots of it and right now. Toshi angled the table with the corner pointing toward the fire. He sat on one side of the table and she at the corner next to him. It brought them closer together. "Let me see what you are working on Jayne."

It was said with such authority, that she felt she needed to do as the teacher instructed. Slowly, she opened her sketch pad to share her work. He eyed a few pages with interest, then opened his book and handed it to her.

"I have an idea Jayne," he told her as he opened the well-worn tin of colored pencils. He laid her sketch pad flat and drew a rough outline of a man. She was instructed to do the same with a woman. The waitress came to the table to take their orders. Jayne kept it simple. "I want a burger with everything on it, a glass of water with lemon, and substitute the fries for a salad."

Toshi ordered a grilled chicken breast with rice and the vegetable of the day along with a pot of hot water for his tea. While they waited for the food to arrive, Toshi took her sketch and began to color in the figure of the woman. Jayne took his pad and began to work on Toshi's sketch. Displeased with his augmentation of the character's breast, she reached over his arm, erased some of the fullness, and redrew in new lines, decreasing the character's bustline from triple E's to a manageable B cup. He in turn erased some of the incorrect lines on the arms of the character, to redefine the pectoral muscles on the man's chest.

From any set of eyes, the two were completely absorbed into what they were doing. To an untrained eye, no one would have known that this was their first time tinkering together as artist. There was no need to explain that to a very surprised Ai, who walked into the restaurant and saw her ex, with a woman who was sketching in his favorite pad. She knew it was his favorite pad because she had given it to him. Ai wondered what else the black woman had been doodling with! Deep breaths were taken as Ai walked across the restaurant to the table, clearing her throat as she approached the couple.

She would not insult the woman by speaking to him in Japanese, because he probably would only answer her in English. "Toshi, what a surprise."

He looked up, unfazed by her sudden appearance, but rose nonetheless to greet her. "Hello, Ai. How are you?"

The woman's eyes were trained on Jayne, who was oblivious to Ai, and focused on the shading techniques she had learned last month at Banzaicon in Toshi's class. If he had not cleared his throat, Jayne probably would not have looked up. "Jayne. This is Ai." He did not give her a label which both women immediately noticed. "Ai, this is Jayne."

Jayne extended a smile at the woman, but did not offer her a handshake. "A pleasure to meet you, Ai." The waitress had returned with the beverages, sitting the mini tea canister of hot water on the table. Ai was still giving Jayne the evil eye but she had dismissed it. There was nothing between her and Toshi. If this woman was of some significance to him, it was his responsibility to qualify why he was having lunch with her.

"Excuse me," Jayne said as she sat back down to the table, remembering the tea he had in his left pocket. *Well, no need to let the water get cold.* Without any thought, she reached into the left pocket of Toshi's jacket that he had draped across the back of the seat, took out the tea, and prepared it as she had seen him do in Columbia. She used his diffuser to place over the top of the cup and slowly poured the hot water over the loose leaves. Toshi had a very wide smile on his face that Ai tried to slap off. "You bastard!"

Toshi caught her hand before it reached his face, lowering Ai's arm back down to her side. "Ai, we are no longer together, you have no need to be upset."

"Did you leave me for this woman, Toshi?"

Jayne looked up, eyes wide with disbelief. The food had arrived and smelled heavenly, shifting Jayne's attention away from Toshi, who surprised Jayne by telling Ai, "Yes I did. Excuse us while we have lunch."

Ai stormed off, furious. Jayne waited for Toshi to be seated. With his head lowered, she was uncertain if he was praying or needed a moment to calm himself, but it only lasted a second. When he cut into his food and took the first bite, Jayne tried to inhale her entire burger. With a mouth full of food and her manners placed in her back pocket, she said "why did you lie to her about us?"

"Who said I lied? He continued to eat his lunch as if nothing had happened. Jayne didn't know what to make of any of it, but Timmy was the priority right now. The poor guy needed to be fed.

The ease of which she conversed with Toshi stunned her. It was very rare that she could sit down with a man and enjoy a meal without the conversation gravitating to something sexual. She was also astounded that he had not hit on her, made a comment about her ass, or even asked for her number. The man didn't even ask if he could friend her on Facebook. As they walked back to where they had parked, he gave her his card. "Call me sometime, Jayne Wright."

He did not wait for a response, but fired up the engine of the sporty car and drove away. Even with her belly full, her mind still went back to him asking that question. *Who said I lied*? He always managed to leave her with something to ponder. At Banzaicon, he told her he had planned to give her hours of pleasure. That simple phrase stuck with her, even today.

She looked down at his card. He was an associate professor at Georgia Regents University. Maybe, if their paths crossed again, she would ante up, and possibly play along. Right now, she was still uncertain, but he was starting to grow on her.

Chapter 6

November sped by as she set the dinner table, sharing Thanksgiving dinner with her grandparents and mother. Her uncle Sydney and his daughter had made it just in time for the cutting of the bird. Her cousin, who was always late, arrived just after the prayer had been said. Prayer.

Had Toshi been praying before he ate the meal? She wasn't sure if Buddhists said a blessing over their food. A modicum of shame coursed through her as she thought about how little she knew of other cultures. Her girlfriend Shannon had dated a Chinese guy once. She at least knew that you poured the tea for the men.

She had done that for Toshi...*after she reached into his jacket pocket to get his tea.* If there was a light bulb over her head, it would be shining brightly right now. That was why Ai believed that something had transpired between them.

Her grandmother was speaking to her and Jayne was in her own head, so much so that Toshi's words, "*who said I lied?*", hit her like a blow to the chest. Had he broken up with Ai after he met her? Wait that would be ridiculous. There was no way to know that he worked in Augusta, let alone that he lived here as well. Running into him in Joann's was weird. She shuddered.

"Chile, don't make me throw this turkey leg at you! You hear me talking to you?" Grandma yelled, staggering Jayne back to reality. Reality was where she needed to be. Toshi Yamaguchi, Associate Professor was the last thing she needed to be thinking about.

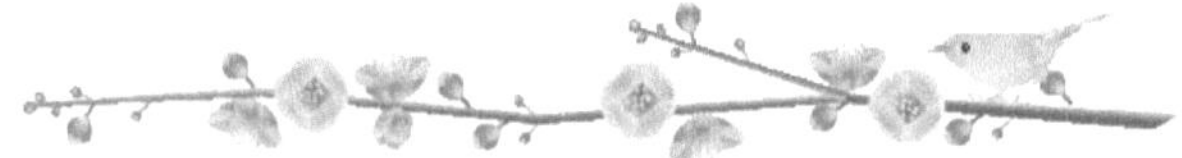

Hirishito Yamaguchi was furious. "What do you mean you broke up with Ai?" His mother had broken into tears, while his sister sat there staring at the really dry turkey his mother had yet again, ruined on Thanksgiving. Why the woman continued to try was beyond him. It was also beyond his comprehension that his father should be so upset.

"I don't love her," was his first tactic.

"A good wife is about more than love Toshi," he exhaled, trying his best to not strangle his oldest child. "Marriage is about building a life together, based on common goals and understanding."

"*Otousan*," he added before going to the second tactic. "That is just it... she doesn't understand me and she never planned to try."

"Toshi," he said with a combination of exasperation, frustration, and disappointment. "Did *you* try? That is what is important."

This conversation needed to end faster than his mother's futile attempt to cook American cuisine. He had saved his ace in the hole for last. "Father. She did not want to leave her job so that we would start our family."

With those words his mother stopped crying and his father looked pensive. Hirishito Yamaguchi owned a chain of Japanese restaurants throughout the southeast. To his credit as a father, neither Toshi nor his sister

Kunio had been made to work in a single one of them. His plans for his children were to be well educated and marry other well educated Japanese Americans. Toshi had become a thorn in his side. It was uncertain if his son would ever settle down, but he wanted grandchildren.

Eri Yamaguchi, with tears dried, sniffled and looked to her husband with pleading eyes. After a deep breath, his father continued with the inquiry. "Ai said you broke up with her to be with a black woman."

His mother burst into tears again and Kunio began to choke. Toshi would have preferred to grade mid-terms than sit through this painful dinner. If he had to undergo this pain, he was not going to be the only one to suffer.

"Father," he said slowly. "Mother," he said even slower. "I did. I am in love with a woman who understands me and I am going to marry her. She just happens to be black."

His mother collapsed onto the plate of cranberry sauce. His father began to curse like a drunken Asian sailor, as his sister broke out into uproarious laughter. Of course, none of it was true, but at least if the door was opened, he could maybe ask Jayne on a date without feeling as if he was ending the continuation of his race. Something inside of him was gravitated toward Jayne. He hoped she would at least call. He wanted to see her again. It was so nice to have a meal with a woman that had something to talk about other than where they were going to build their house, money, or what new outfit she just purchased. Even more so, the third beauty to Jayne was that she was an artist and a good one. Her ass was her first and those luscious lips were second and last.

For the first time in his life, he found himself waiting and hoping for a woman to call him. The other woman who was unrelenting on him mentally, in the same instance, was his mother, who was still pressing her face into the cranberry sauce. His parents would be fine, in time. Jayne may not be the woman for him, but he at least deserved an opportunity to find out. His journey into the play arena of happiness was costly, but he had to start somewhere.

Chapter 7

December waltzed in with little flourish. Bringing only a few cold breezes as it kicked off the winter season. Jayne had thought of Toshi several times, but had misplaced the business card he had given her. *Oh well, it probably was for the best anyway.*

The past three weeks she had spent working on her Misty Knight costume for the Atlanta Comic Convention. When she looked on the website and found out that people who attended in costume got in free, she was all for it. With the new design on her comic book and using the techniques she had learned from Toshi, the book looked good. This was her opportunity to rub elbows with some really great comic artists and hopefully move her comic book series forward.

Her Grammy was still upset that she was running off, unchaperoned again to a convention that was rife with horny men looking to take advantage of a respectable young woman. Again, she was given the *watch what you drink* speech, and the *keep an eye on your food* lecture, because her grandmother was convinced that at conferences, men slipped women mickeys, and would then have their way with their unconscious body. She had never heard of such a thing, but nonetheless, she kept her eyes peeled.

The Comic Convention was not an all-day event, which made it easy for Jayne to leave Augusta, take I-20 into Atlanta and head up 1-85 to the Marriott on Century. She wore the second skin red catsuit, that had open sides and her favorite smoothed out push up bra. When she stepped out of the car, she donned the red ankle boots, strapped on the gun holster, and slid her toy Berretta into the slot. The afro wig went on last, right before the red leather gloves and the Velcro Bionic pieces. There was no contest to be judged here, but Jayne was a firm believer that if you were going to be a bad ass, go full throttle.

She entered the hotel to be greeted by her people. Other women were also dressed as powerful agents of change. Men, armored to defend our way of life. Artists who created new worlds to inspire imagination and thousands of fans who appreciated the hard work. Conventions were a place that Jayne felt she could be herself.

The white leather satchel which held her sketch book was slung across her shoulder, with the strap falling between her breasts. Several men showed an appreciation of her assets and attempted to make conversation. What they wanted to talk about was not her costume, but what was in it. *Pigs*. One eager nerd actually had the nerve to reach his hand out and try and touch her body. Jayne drew her Berretta, stayed in character, while using what she thought would be the perfect Misty Knight voice. “Don’t make me shoot you sucka!”

As the afternoon waned, disappointment crept in that she had driven two hours to Atlanta and had not made a single connection. The artists were self-centered, the attendees were more collectors who wanted an item for the value, or to say that they owned it, and no one seemed to be very appreciative of anything. It was a busted trip.

Timmy had started to growl at her, but all she wanted

was to hit the road and go home. It was a few minutes after five as she headed toward the parking garage to find her car. The sound of a familiar voice brought an unwilling smile to her face. She peered around the corner to see Toshi talking to three men. In the middle of them both was a very "out of it" blond woman dressed as Rogue.

The guys were telling Toshi to mind his own business, but dressed as a young Master Izo, in traditional Japanese garb, he was not backing down. Jayne strained her ear to hear more. "Gentlemen, the lady is in no shape to make any decisions."

"We are just going to take her to her room. She is a friend of ours." The small one in the back with the shifty eyes told Toshi.

Toshi did not accuse them of anything, but only added, "I have a sister and I would hate to think if she was in this state that someone would not look out for her."

The guys were not about to give up their easy prize. The big one on the right made a move toward Toshi who did not flinch, but remained firm. "Are you seriously going to attempt to fight me, so that you can take this woman?"

It was said with such incredulity that the second guy in the group, turned and left, telling his two friends, "I'm outta here." The others were still standing there. The bigger of the two obviously had something to prove, but so did Toshi.

"If you make a move, I am going to hurt you." He slightly adjusted his feet like she had seen so many times in Kung Fu movies. "If by chance you two do over power me, you realize what that would make you."

The smaller man, with his jaw still agape as if to catch

wayward flies, answered with, "what?"

Toshi still did not flinch as the woman collapsed in front of him and hurled up chunks of whatever she had eaten. "It would make you a rapist." The second man scrunched his face and without saying a word to his friend, turned and left.

"Which leaves just you big guy," Toshi told him. "Seriously. Is it worth it when there are so many willing women here, just waiting for a big strapping fellow like you to come and please them?" Jayne watched the guy's shoulder's drop along with his defenses. Eventually, he conceded. "Help me get her up and to the front desk."

Jayne backed up around the corner, as the two men carried the very lucky woman to the main lobby reception area. The clerk, along with two other women helped her up to her room.

Toshi shook the big guy's hand and thanked him for his assistance. Jayne walked up. "Way to go Master Izo."

Toshi's face lit up when he saw her standing there. Instead of greeting her with warm and fuzzy feelings he said, "give me your phone."

"Good to see you too, Toshi."

"Yeah, yeah, give me your phone." Reluctantly she reached into the bag and removed her iPhone, giving it to him. He unlocked the phone, went to contacts and added his name, number and snapped a photo of himself before giving it back to her. Inside the inner pocket of his gi and removed his phone, handing it to her. "Put your number in there."

"What if I don't want to?"

He paused for a minute, lowered his defenses, and took

a different approach with her. "Then I would be devastated Jayne Wright." He flashed a set of teeth that were well maintained. She knew she was being given a line, but he had delivered it so perfectly.

She unlocked his phone, went to contacts and added her name and number. "A cool chick like me wouldn't want something like that on her conscious."

Toshi stood there watching her in the tight red pants, silly afro wig, fake gun and ridiculous boots. He never thought he had seen a more stunning woman. It bothered him how much he wanted her. It felt disturbing that it was taking every bit of his resolve to not pull her into his arms and whisper sweet words of eroticism into her ear until she surrendered to him. He made eye contact with her as she typed in her number, forcing himself to not gaze at the sexy thighs that he wanted to feel wrapped tightly around his waist. She smiled at him when she handed him back his phone. Those beautiful full lips beckoning him for a kiss.

"Dude, you okay? You got this strange look on your face."

The phone was slipped back into his gi. "I was just debating on getting a room or making the drive back tonight." He wanted to ask if he got the room, would she stay with him, but he had tried the direct approach with her and it had not worked before.

"Oh, okay. I am driving back tonight." She looked at her watch. "Speaking of which, I need to get going." On cue, Timmy started to growl.

"Will you have dinner with me before you go Jayne," he asked nearly breaking into a sweat as he held his tongue.

"Naw. I'll grab something quick on the way." She was about to leave, but thought about him stepping in to save that woman from a very bad evening. "You have the number, so call me sometime."

Blood raced through his veins and coursed up to his ears, as he mentally willed the red liquid of life to not head toward his nether regions. Again, he found himself losing the battle with his will, as he watched that perfect ass walk away from him for the third time. She must have known he was watching, as she looked at him over her shoulder. "Stop watching my ass Toshi Yamaguchi!" Jayne added a little extra sashay as she made her way to the elevator.

Toshi broke into a wide grin. Jayne Wright had managed to get under his skin. She had walked up to the counter, threw down some bills, and said she was ready to play. This was going to be a problem.

Chapter 8

It was a cool, crisp December wind that blew across Toshi's face as he exited his car to enter the Kroger on Washington Road. The sky was as grey as his mood leaving him with riddled with melancholy. This would be the first Christmas that he would be single. Based on his current mindset, it would be the last. He had never considered himself a man that constantly needed the company of a woman to feel as if his life had meaning or purpose, but cooking dinner for one on Christmas Eve took him to a new low.

Earlier in the day, he had gone to his parent's to spend some time, but the disappointment on both of their faces was too much to process. It only exacerbated the totality of his failure when his sister, Kunio showed up with her new boyfriend. The fat headed doctor. Toshi hated him already.

The other thing he was hating was the start of the rain. The large droplets pelted his head, as he made his way through the main doors and grabbed a hand cart to purchase a few food items. Christmas dinner would be at his parents, but he opted not to stay the night. He lied to them about having plans. His mother began to cry again, as his father patted her on the back to console her. Irony was a mean mistress. His mother was devastated that her son was involved with a woman, who in actuality, wouldn't even give him the time of day. Maybe this was his penance for being a scoundrel in college.

As he made his way to the meat department, he first

stopped in the produce section to pick up some leeks, Chinese cabbage, carrots, and an eggplant. In the meat department he looked closely at the salmon. Not many of the packages looked very fresh. He reached for the one in the back, but a hand slapped his and snatched it out of the way. Toshi turned to see Jayne standing there. “This is my dinner.”

Her smile was so warm and inviting, that Toshi swore he heard music playing in the background. “Well, since we were thinking of having the same thing for dinner, will you allow me to cook it for you?”

A man offering to cook dinner? For her? That was a first. “Sure,” she said and put the salmon in his basket.

“Oh, I have to buy it as well?”

Jayne touched the upper portion of her teeth with her tongue. “You were going to buy it anyway. How about I buy the wine?”

“Deal,” he told her as she eyed his basket, asking if they needed anything else.

Toshi wondered if she lived close by. “Jayne. My place or yours?”

The look she gave him was one of concern that Toshi staved off by adding, “At my place, I have rice, seasonings, and everything else to go with the meal. I am not sure what you have.” He watched her relax.

Her hand flew to her face. “Wait! I can’t have dinner with you tonight!” It felt like a blow to his chest. “I rode my bike to the store, so I can’t follow you to your place.”

“Jayne, I will take you home after dinner.” Toshi was obviously not understanding why she felt this was some form of a dilemma.

"I need my own car, in case I have to leave in a hurry, or you get fresh." Her hand was on her hip. His father had taught his sister the same rule, so he understood.

"If you are on your bike, you must live close by. So do I." he thought about the weather. "Besides, it has started to rain, so I will need to give you a ride anyway. You can put away your groceries and follow me to my place, or I can just cook at yours." He was not going to let her get away from him again. The thought of being alone tonight also hung in the recesses of his mind.

"Jayne." He said her name softly. "It's Christmas Eve and I would rather not eat alone." The words had rolled out of his mouth so easily that he looked around the store to make sure he was the one who had actually said it.

"Neither do I," she told him as she touched his hand. "Come on doc. Timmy will be waking up soon, so let's get this dinner thing started."

The checkout was quick. Toshi had her wait under the covering while he retrieved his car. He lowered the back seat and slid her bike into the hatchback alongside the groceries. Jayne was impressed Toshi used his umbrella to escort her around the car. He even opened the door, closing it once she was inside.

He slid into the driver seat and put the car into gear. "Which way?"

"I live pretty close by, hence the bike." She gave him directions out of the parking lot. Making a left on Alexander Drive and then driving less than a mile down the hill. "These apartment homes on the left is me," she told him as she gave him instructions on how to access the security gate.

Instead of pulling into the visitor's lane, he pulled into the resident side. Jayne felt silly. "Oh, you are right. I do have my access card."

Toshi said nothing as he rolled down the window, reached up into the visor and removed a card that slid into the slot opening the gate. Jayne's jaw dropped. "You live in this complex too?"

"I do, but I live in building 200. Which building is yours?" He tried to sound casual as he toyed with either his luck, or fate playing a cruel game.

"I live in the back, in the 800 building," she told him in a lowered voice. Jayne's mind was running amok with the probability of all this. Instead of avoiding and fighting Toshi, maybe she needed to find out why they were constantly being brought together.

"Let's secure your bike first, put away your items, and we will drive around to my building."

Jayne did not allow him to come all the way into her apartment, but only allowed him to place the groceries in the kitchen. She quickly put away what needed refrigeration. The other items, she left in the bag.

"I'm ready." She grabbed her keys and followed him down the stairs. The roles were reversed as she watched the back of him walk with such confidence, grace, and almost a quiet stealth. His bearing was almost regal as he descended the stairwell, walking her to her car, and closing her door, before getting into his own.

Jayne trailed him back to the front of the complex, coming around the side of the structures to building 200. She breathed deeply as she took the second bag from his vehicle and trailed him up the first set of stairs to the back of his building. The keys jangled as he opened the door to permit her entry into his private world.

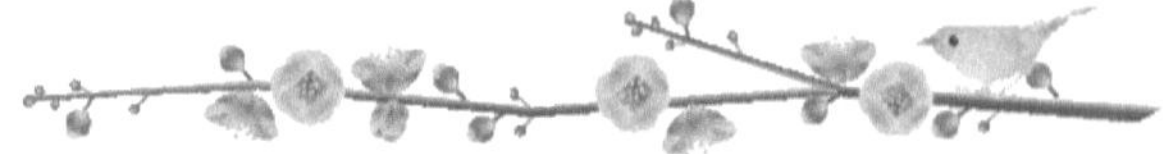

"Here, let me take your jacket." Toshi helped remove her jacket as he locked the door, removed his shoes, and set about prepping dinner. "Excuse me for a second," he told her as he took off his jacket as well, while walking down the hallway to his bedroom. Jayne craned her neck to the right to see where he had went, silently praying that he did not return wearing just a smoking jacket and a smile. She did as she saw him do and removed her shoes before stepping onto the carpet.

Then there was the flush of the commode, the start of the faucet, and seconds thereafter, the man himself returned to the kitchen. The look on her face amused him. "You thought I was going to come back out in a smoking jacket and some drawstring pants didn't you?"

She chuckled a little. "Yeah. I was worried for a minute there."

"I invited you for dinner Jayne," he told her. He poured a glass of wine for them both and washed the rice for the steamer.

Jayne, with wine glass in hand, walked around the apartment and was surprised to find that he had three bedrooms. She pointed to the third door, asking his permission. She lost her breath when she saw it was a full studio, with drawing tables, a sewing machine, a serger, and sketches posted to corkboards. She wanted to take out her pencils, sit down, and began to draw a masterpiece. The walls were painted a soft taupe with large cork billboards extending from the ceiling on three of the walls. The fourth wall was a window, which shone light directly onto the artist table.

She heard the sizzle of meat, the knife striking the cutting board, and water being run over vegetables through a colander. Those sounds she knew well. Toshi remained quiet as she went to the second door, once more checking for his approval before opening it. Inside, she was pleased to see it was a Zen space with nothing more than a slant board, a cd player, and a yoga mat. One wall was painted a soft pink with Japanese cherry blossom appliques on the wall. The third door was his bedroom. A door that was left slightly ajar from when he left the restroom earlier.

"So, this is the dragon's lair, where the damsels are all brought to the slaughter," she said aloud as she peered inside the room.

"You do have a flair for the dramatic. You know that right?"

Jayne didn't quite know why she was surprised when she looked inside the bedroom, but she was. It was so basic. It looked as if he had just moved in. He took minimalism to a new level. The queen size bed had a simple red quilt and two large pillows; one of which looked well used. Jayne figured that was the one he slept on. The night stands held nothing personal, nor the walls. There was no television or family photos. "Toshi, no TV?"

"The bedroom is for sleeping, making love, and creating life. I watch TV on the couch."

Alarms were buzzing in Jayne's head as she looked about the place. "So, do you do this often? Cook for women?" She stopped herself from saying anything more.

"Actually, you are only the third woman I have brought here. Fourth if you include my mother." She watched him dice the eggplant with the skill of a chef.

Seated at the counter, her eyes ventured to the countertop where he had lined up small bowls in which to serve the dishes he was preparing.

"Am I the first black woman?" she asked softly, almost speaking the words into the glass.

"The first one I brought here, yes." He looked up at her and smiled.

"I can take that so many ways, Toshi. I mean did you just move in?" She paused. "What are we talking about here…?"

He saw no need to be dishonest with her today or any other day. "I have lived here for almost two years. To answer the question you are trying to find a way to ask me, I have dated black women."

"Oh, I see," she said as she took plates to the dining table.

"You see what?" He followed behind her with a serving tray with fresh sliced ginger, two rice bowls, and the serving plate of the salmon and vegetables.

"So, you have a thing for black women." She almost said it with disgust.

He pulled out her chair, helped her be seated, and then laid a cloth napkin across her lap. His fingers gently grazing her arm. "No Jayne. I have a thing for you."

He took his seat and saw the wide grin on her face.

Jayne had to give it to him. "That was pretty smooth, Toshi."

"You think so?" As she nodded, he agreed with her. "Yeah, that one was pretty good." He laughed a bit, keeping his eyes on her.

Despite so many misgivings and a really rough start, she liked him. The subtle scent of him in the bedroom was so faint, but potent, that her senses had fired up the moment she saw the indentation in the pillow where his head rested every night. The smell was stronger as he sat closer.

"Toshi," she said. Timmy made his presence known, growling loudly. "What are we doing?"

He pulled the large plate with vegetables between the two of them. "I am having dinner on Christmas Eve with a friend. What are you doing?"

"Just a friend?"

Toshi added a little more wine to her glass, then his own. "Jayne, I like you, your spirit, and your energy. If what we have is nothing more than friendship, I can accept that, but it is nice to have a conversation with a woman who understands what I am talking about."

"So, what you are saying is that I am safe." She was eyeing the food.

"I am not understanding what you mean." He honestly did not.

"I mean, if I eat this food and drink this wine, are you going to put on some soft music, a porn tape, and jump me?"

"Not unless you want me to, Jayne." He used the back end of his chopsticks to serve her food. "I am a simple man. If I invite you for dinner, we have dinner. If I want you to come over for something more, I will make it clear in the invitation."

Jayne would not let it go. It could not be that simple, especially considering their first couple of conversations. If life had taught her anything, it was to not let down your guard. The feeling that was circling the drain of concern, was he was trying a new tactic. She blurted it out with no regard for consequence. "Are you saying, you no longer want to have sex with me?"

He stopped chewing and swallowed hard, laid down his chopsticks. Jayne shrank back a little. "If you said to me…" he used a girlie voice, "…*Toshi, take me right now.* I would have to cook you a new dinner." He watched her face before he delivered the blow. "I would clear this table and you would have rice, eggplant, and steamed veggies all in your hair and ass." Jayne's mouth dropped, as he looked at her with a straight face. "I would go hard too Jayne! I would go hard! I would get all Super Saiyan on you," he told her as he started making the anime faces, with noises of "grrr, ahhh, ooooh".

She could not help it. She burst into laughter. Toshi was laughing as well. A deep belly gut type of laughter, but he paused, becoming serious again before passing her a bowl of rice. "Tonight, I wish nothing more than the pleasure of your company." To his shock, it was the truth. "However, to answer your question, no. I no longer want to have sex with you." Her face lost its expression. "I would at some point, relish the moment when I can make love to you." The idea of getting her into bed tonight had not crossed his mind.

She was grinning, "That was pretty smooth too. I like that one even more."

Toshi watched her relax and changed the subject by telling her, "so in Japanese culture, before a meal you say, *itadakimasu,* meaning I gratefully receive, before you commence eating." Jayne repeated after him asking what is said once the meal was complete. "After dinner, to say thank you for the meal, you will say *gochisosama."* She repeated after him again. "I would then respond, *deshita."*

She tasted the food. "This is amazing, Toshi."

He found himself beaming with pride as she raved over every vegetable cut, the rice, and especially the salmon. There were so many more things he was looking forward to teaching Jayne Wright and in his immediate thoughts, none were related to having her in his bed. It was a weird feeling, but one, Toshi felt that he liked. If it cost a bit more time to earn her trust, then he would gladly pay it, with interest.

Chapter 9

Jayne woke up feeling a new energy. Dinner with Toshi had been a pleasant surprise and she had truly enjoyed the evening. After she helped wash the dishes, he made them cups of tea as they discussed some of the drawings in his office on the board. The conversation turned toward different mediums for achieving certain artistic effects with charcoals, colored pencils, and acrylics. As much as she hated to admit, he was correct. It was wonderful talking to someone who understood what you were talking about. What she was reluctant to admit even more, was her attraction to him.

At 11:45 he walked her downstairs to her car. The fob was used to open the door. She leaned against her vehicle to tell him she had a good time. He leaned down to open the door and she mistook it for him leaning in for a kiss. It was too late to take it back. Their lips connected, but he did not pull away. Instead, he placed his hands on either side of her on the roof of the car, and deepened the kiss. Jayne's mouth opened as his tongue darted inside to mate with hers. Her hands slipped inside his jacket, as she allowed her nails to graze his back when she grabbed handfuls of his cotton shirt. It had been so long since she felt the weight of a man. She pulled him forward, taking all of his weight onto her body as he pressed her against the car. A slight moan escaped her throat and she felt his growing desire pressed against her belly. His kiss deepened still, until she felt him pulling away. The cool air between them served as a wake up. Under the soft glow of the street light, Toshi saw the raw passion in her eyes and his blood begin to boil.

A feeble attempt to say her name was halted as his voice came out all raspy. He tried again. “Jayne get in the car.”

Her fingers touched his chest and trailed down his stomach, feeling the muscles of his abdomen under the shirt. Before her hand could go any lower, he grabbed it, pressing it to her side, placing a softer kiss on her lips. “Get in the car Jayne.” Toshi physically pushed her into the seat and closed the car door. “Text me when you get home.” He remained only long enough to hear her start the engine and put the car into gear.

The next morning, her mind was full of the thoughts of *what if* he had taken her by the hand back into his place. She would have made a fool of herself. “Crap, I forgot to text him last night.” Already dressed for church, she looked for her purse. She had forgotten that as well. It must still be at his place.

Toshi woke up slowly faced with the harsh reality that what he was holding was not Jayne, but a pillow. He kicked himself several times last night for not taking advantage of the circumstance and drug her back into his place to make love to her all night. She had been willing to give him her body, but he wanted something else. The word to define what he wanted could not be formulated, but it was hanging about his frontal lobe. A loud groan rumbled from his groin, up through his gut, to his stomach, and out of his mouth.

A light tapping was heard at the front door. He jumped up quickly thinking maybe Jayne had come back and was ready to make love this morning. Heaven knows he was. He opened the door to find Kunio, his sister standing there. He groaned again as she entered the apartment.

“Merry Happy Ho-Ho to you too big brother.” She kicked off her shoes and sat the bags down she had brought over. “I brought you breakfast and came to make sure you are not late for church, again.”

Toshi peered in the bag, frowning at her selection. He did not like deep fried food, nor was he particularly fond of biscuits. “Toshi, hit the shower. I will make some tea while you get dressed.” She pushed at his shoulders trying to get him moving. “You could at least say good morning to me.”

He kissed her on the forehead, groaned again, and headed toward the shower. Kunio called after him, “and brush those teeth while you are at it. Smells like you had some bad fish for dinner.”

She heard the shower start and set about making tea, but was interrupted by a light tap at the door. Uncertain if her brother was expecting anyone, she answered the knocking to find a black woman standing there. Ai had not been lying and Toshi hadn’t said it to piss off their parents. Her brother could actually be dating this woman.

“I’m sorry. Is Toshi home?” Jayne asked as she eyed the beautiful Japanese woman.

“Yes, please come in.” Kunio stepped aside to allow Jayne entry into the apartment.

Jayne wasn't sure who the woman was and decided to err on the side of caution. "I left my bag here yesterday and just came to get it."

The beautiful woman used her right hand as an answer to go ahead and get what she needed. Jayne removed her shoes before stepping onto the carpet. Kunio knew then, she had been here before.

"I am Kunio," she said as she watched Jayne's expressions.

"I am Jayne. A friend of Toshi's." She rounded the corner and found her purse on the couch. "Here it is. I will be on my way." She thanked the lady and at the same time heard the shower stop. Toshi called out, "Kunio, are you making us some tea?"

"I am and you have a guest out here," she yelled back, eyes still fixed on Jayne. Kunio wanted to see the interaction between her brother and this woman.

Toshi nearly ran from the bedroom, his dress slacks halfway wedged into his underwear, chest still wet as he pulled a wife beater over his head. Jayne lowered her gaze as he straightened his clothing, attempting to sound casual. "I left my bag yesterday with my cell phone in it. Hence, no text message." She said each section of words slowly hoping it would explain why she had not texted him last night.

A bevy of emotions flooded through his mind thinking if his sister wasn't here, they could they pick up where they left off last night. Before he could speak, Kunio broke the staring match between them. "Good grief Toshi! If we are late for church, mom and dad are going to be furious."

"Jayne. Do you have a little sister?" he asked as he

dashed back into the room to retrieve his shirt and tie. "If not, would you like one?"

He buttoned his shirt and Jayne, without thinking, stepped forward and began to fix his tie in a Windsor knot. She said in a low voice, "do you have plans for New Year's Eve?"

Toshi, adjusted his shirt into his pants. "No. What do you have in mind?"

"I was thinking, if you came over, I could return the favor and make dinner for you."

A faint smile crept into the corners of his mouth. "I would like that. I would like that a lot, Jayne."

"Great six o'clock. Bring the champagne," she said as she adjusted the narrow end of the fabric.

Kunio strained to hear what was being said, until Jayne suddenly turned, startling her. "A pleasure to meet you Kunio."

Toshi needed to make sure last night wasn't a fluke. He called her name as she reached the door. When Jayne turned, he grabbed a fistful of the front of her coat pulling her to him. He awaited her smile before lowering his head to give her a light kiss. "Thank you."

"*Dou itashimashite*, Toshi."

After Jayne left, Toshi sat at the counter attempting to choke down the greasy biscuit with overly salted ham. Kunio wasn't sure if he was hating it or loving it, because he was doing it all with a weird smile on his face. He had kissed the woman and was now smiling.

"Why are you staring at me Kunio?"

"You are smiling," she said as she poured him more tea.

"Yeah. What's the big deal?"

She poured herself another cup. "I just don't remember the last time I saw you smile, that's all."

Chapter 10

Christmas was always a sad time around Jayne's house. It was her least favorite holiday, followed closely by Valentine's Day. A celebration that was a waste of marketing revenue. What she did love about the Christmas season was the great sales which took place afterwards. Being employed in the advertising industry, she fully understood that companies had to sell any excess Christmas items before a certain time to avoid paying the extra taxes. Once she hipped her friends to this knowledge, it became their thing after the holiday to spend a day shopping.

Brionna, Tamika, and RaShunda had been her closest friends since high school. Between the four of them, it was often joked that they could have their own reality show since each of them represented the quintessential definition of the stereotypical black woman. What saddened them all, as the punch line of the joke, was that none had a successful relationship.

Jayne had a steady boyfriend for about a year, but he attempted several times to control everything she did, wore, and even dreamed. Grandma Pearl told her that most black women often settled for a piece of man, because they were unwilling to wait for the right man. "Sugar Pie," Grammy told her. "If you are a good woman, you need a good man. Wait for God to send you the right one, instead of going with *just* anyone." She followed her advice and let George, her second real boyfriend, go his own way. Of course, her girlfriends didn't understand how she could let that fine ass brother go, but they didn't see the real George. They saw the George who drove the Mercedes and wore designer clothes with fancy wrist watches. George also never appealed to her sexually, which is why Alex was the only man she that had been intimately involved. No one ever saw the controlling George who talked to her like she was stupid or the George who made fun of her desire to be a graphic novelist. Brionna often teased her, saying that she had become that sister who didn't trust men and would rather read about love than try to live it.

For Jayne that was the pot, sitting on the roof, yelling at the kettle, "Hey Homie. Did you know you were black?" Brionna was the type of sister who was in love with the idealism of the concept of love. Every other year she would have a new man. Pitiful men who required a great deal of fixing up to even be presentable among good honest folk. Brionna's latest was Tyrone Jenkins. A man she bragged that worked for the city and was on his way up. Jayne remained quiet when she found out the stinking truth about Tyrone's good paying job. A smile, a hug, and agreement with Brionna was in order, because Tyrone worked hanging off the back of a garbage truck. Which in all honesty, left him nowhere to go, but up. Jayne never uttered a word to her friend that she knew what Tyrone did for living. Truth in context, was harsher than truth in reality. There wasn't a darn thing wrong with the brother earning an honest living, especially considering the alternative of what he could be doing. With his job, he did as a man should do and helped to take care of his woman.

Tamika, on the other hand, always looked for the man who would take care of her completely. Jayne categorized her friend as the type of sister whose weave was always right, nails were done, and wore the latest and hippest clothing. Any man who came within nose shot of her could smell the money dripping from her haute couture. If he desired a sniff, he had to come with at least a platinum line of credit or he could stay where he was. The drawback to her lifestyle was that the men that were in the position to take care of her, often belonged to another woman. The woman who helped put him through graduate school. The woman that ate ramen noodles two nights a week so that he would have a nice suit for job interviews, to get that first great job. The woman who bore his children and sat up with them at night doing homework while her husband was out doing Tamika. Yes, she was the type of woman who did not care, as long as she felt she was in control.

Control was an odd thing. Jayne often found that whenever a person felt they had it all together and everything was under control which was the moment in life where everything was just the opposite. RaShunda lived the example.

A college graduate with a specialization in marketing and promotions, RaShunda obtained a cushy job with a local Fortune 500 company and was on the move. Jayne labeled her friend as the angry black woman. In sincerity, she did it to herself. Grandma Pearl's rule of thumb was, you never poop where you eat. RaShunda made the mistake of dating a coworker. Not only did she date a coworker, but it was a man who worked in her department and was her equal. Being the loudmouth braggart that she is, RaShunda had to share everything that came into her head; her time of month, the sandwich she ate giving her gas, and her latest really cute marketing idea. It was no real surprise to anyone when Calvin took her ad campaign, dressed it up, and presented it as his own. The campaign made the company millions. Calvin was promoted and sent to head up a division at the corporate headquarters in Switzerland. RaShunda became resentful. Scratch that, she became vindictive. During the first round of cutbacks and layoffs on her job, she was the first to be let go.

It took three years of therapy, personal coaching, and another shot at the big leagues before she settled down and became tolerable again. Jayne wondered if the last set back was ever going to make her friend right in the head again. Her latest setback was marriage. A marriage to the wrong man. RaShunda married a man who seemed to dote on her and give her everything she needed; love and support, but not a lot of understanding. Ronnie's lack of understanding of what she did for a living manifested itself in his funky attitude when RaShunda took a client to dinner. It was even worse when *his wife* had to work late or received a gift from a client. Ronnie took it over the top when RaShunda earned a sizeable bonus that enabled her to put a hefty down payment on a new car that she desperately needed.

Jayne sat across the table from her three gal pals and refused to buy into any of the drama. RaShunda started the conversation, complaining as usual about her husband. The anger simmering underneath her mantle. “Would you believe that fool wanted me to take back my car? He don’t know who he is dealing with if he expects that.....”

Tamika ignored her. Too busy pushing lettuce leaves about her plate, while eyeing the new two carat diamond on her finger. Jayne wanted to ask whose husband had given her that, but the conversation was turned instead by Brionna who flashed the new quarter carat diamond ring she was sporting on her left hand.

“Girl, marriage ain’t nothing but a trap. You should be smart and give it back and enjoy your freedom like Jayne over here,” RaShunda blurted out, smashing Brionna’s joy. Tamika, being trifling as usual, compared her new sizable ring to the baby carat that Brionna was attempting to flash. Jayne was the stabilizer of the group.

“How wonderful for you and Tyrone, Bri. Congrats.” Everyone relaxed a bit. “Let’s order a round a margaritas to toast the upcoming nuptials.” The waiter took the order and returned shortly with four glasses.

Jayne’s joy didn’t go unnoticed by RaShunda’s harsh eyes. “Who is he Jayne?”

“I’m sorry. Who is who?”

“Don’t play coy Honey. Who is this man you are seeing?”

This caught the attention of Tamika and Brionna who both focused in on Jayne. “I thought I noticed something different about her as well,” Brionna added.

“Did you finally find someone to dust the cobwebs off that sealed up pocketbook, girl?” Tamika burst into laughter at her own question as she dug at Jayne's celibacy.

"No one is sticking their fingers in my pocketbook," Jayne said with ease. The margaritas arrived and she began to pour. "Besides, I would rather have dust on it than more fingerprints than the bathroom door at Walmart!"

Balance had been restored as the ladies laughed at the dig, but RaShunda knew that Jayne had avoided the question. For Jayne, there was no real answer. She and Toshi had only shared two kisses and two meals. There was some chemistry between them, but too many differences which could not easily be overlooked. Her focus centered on her and Toshi getting through New Year's Eve tomorrow night with her panties on and intact. The rest, she would deal with later.

Chapter 11

Raheem, Felix and Phở sat in the Mexican restaurant laughing and having a good conversation with their friend Toshi. The four had been friends since ninth grade math club at Lakeside High School. Each man was successful in his own field, but Felix was the only one who was married.

Felix Masterson, the science genius had come from a meager background and was that student who lived in the trailer park close to the school. The ongoing joke between them was that Felix used his knowledge of science to create drugs in the '90s that helped him create a slush fund for college. His parents, both hard working people, had no idea what he had been up to. The saving grace was his grades that, along with some help from Toshi, earned him a full scholarship to Princeton. Felix returned home when his parents became ill. He took a job with a local pharmaceutical company and took a major cut in his salary, but he was still happy. His wife Jenny, was a really sweet woman, who looked forward to giving him a home full of squalling blonde children.

Raheem Thomas, on the other hand, lived a different lifestyle. He was shocked when in the eleventh grade he *came out* to his friends. None of the group seemed to care since they always knew and it had no real bearing on how they regarded their friend. The friendship meant everything to Raheem, whose father suffered a heart attack when he learned of his son's sexual orientation.

His father's love for his son was not diminished, especially when Raheem's sister began popping out babies, year after year. Finally after child number six, Mr. Thomas asked the doctors to tie her tubes. There was no disappointing his parents when their very large, burly son, who had grown a full beard at the age of 15, received his acceptance letter to Harvard. He had a partial scholarship, but with a supplemental scholarship from Hirishito's Steak House and one from King's Beauty Supply, he made it through the first year, earning more scholarships. Dr. Raheem Thomas came home to take an Assistant Dean position at Paine College in the math department.

Nguyễn Hàn Phở held an MBA and was also a Yale graduate like Toshi. As the eldest son, a few years back, he took over his family's beauty supply stores and nail salons, doubling the profit margin and retiring his parents. It was no secret that under his skin, he resented a $150,000 dollar education that was used to make sure plus sized women were pleased when his employees asked, "*you want design?*" He also felt some resentment toward Toshi who never had to work in his family's restaurants. His friend Toshi never came home from work smelling like Hirishito's secret sauce. He would come home smelling like nail acrylic and hair weave. The resentment didn't go very far when he came to terms with no longer having a student loan, his BMW was paid for and he'd made a sizeable cash deposit on his five bedroom home on Stallings Island.

All in all, they were good guys and really good friends who truly understood the strength and weaknesses of each member of the group.

"Hey you," a sweet voice said. Toshi looked up and saw Jayne standing there. A huge grin covered his face as he rose to greet the woman who was costing him a few sleepless nights. He embraced her as if he had not seen her in a year. He closed his eyes as he inhaled her subtle fragrance; something his friends easily noticed. With his arm still about her shoulders, he turned Jayne to face his friends.

"Jayne," he said as he looked down at her upturned face. "This is Raheem, Phở, and Felix. Guys, this is Jayne."

She was surprised when each man rose and shook her hand. A bigger surprise was the diversity of the group. Toshi asked, "are you here alone? You are more than welcome to join us."

Jayne was about to turn and point to the table where her friends were sitting, but her hand came into contact with RaShunda's boobs. Her friends were all standing behind her. They were scrutinizing Toshi, who had yet to remove his arm from around her shoulders. Jayne cleared her throat. "These are my friends."

"This is Rashunda," who added an "hmmmnnhhn," with a sister girl neck roll. "Tamika," who instantly asked what Toshi did for a living. And Brionna, who spontaneously felt the need to say, "look at you with your own little Rainbow Coalition over here."

Jayne let out a large swoosh of air followed by laughter as she introduced Toshi's friends to the group. Brionna's eyes first went to Raheem, then to Felix, and eventually settled on Phở, who looked over his shoulder to see who she was staring at. When his eyes came back front, he realized that Brionna was eyeing him. Just to be certain, he looked over the other shoulder. Nope. No one was behind him.

Jayne sensed Phở's discomfort. "Well, it was nice to meet you all." She patted Toshi on the chest, but his arm tightened about her shoulders. He had kissed her in front of his sister. He needed to know if Jayne would acknowledge him in front of all of their friends. He looked down at her, as she leaned upward and placed a feathery kiss upon his lips. "See you tomorrow night. Don't forget the Champagne."

There.

It was tangible.

It was in the open.

Toshi sat down at the table with three sets of eyes affixed on him. "What?"

Phở was the first to say something. "He's smiling."

This remark was followed by Felix. "He closed his eyes when he hugged her."

Raheem was the last to weigh in. "She seems so nice and normal Toshi. What is she doing with you?

Toshi was offended. "What do you mean Raheem?" He also addressed the other comments. "I smile all the time." He paused. "What do you mean, I closed my eyes?"

All three men were shaking their heads in unison, telling him no, but Toshi was not hearing it. "I don't like the implications here fellas."

Raheem spoke up. "Let's see. There was Cindy, Candy, Karla, Mandy Rae, Jaqueeda, Gloria, Bronetta, Jonqueeta, Melissa Ann...."

"What are you trying to say Raheem? That I am some kind of dog?"

Phở spoke up. "No Toshi. You are a wolf. An insatiable wolf that stalks and hunts all the time. Women are not safe around you. You go through them and toss the scraps aside."

Toshi was getting angry. "That is not true."

"Dude, I was your college roommate. There was always different women in and out of your bed. At one point, I thought your dick was going to go on strike for being overworked," Phở said with a straight face.

Felix added his two cents. "She seems like a really sweet woman Toshi."

"She is. I really like her," Toshi said in his defense. "I don't just toss women aside!" He needed his friends to understand. "There is a red hot fire burning inside of me. I need the right woman to make it burn blue. You know what I am saying?"

Raheem would not let it go. "Do you like her, like her?" Which was a running joke in high school. They all knew Toshi never stayed with one woman for long. "Besides, your parents would have a cow."

Toshi sipped at his tea. "They already know."

Phở was shaking his head. He had come home once with a white girl and his parents treated him as if he had picked up the local crack head. He could only imagine how Toshi's parents had reacted.

"My father went into one of his speeches. My sister choked on some of my Mother's burnt turkey." He told his friends.

"What did your Mother do?" Felix asked.

"She passed out in the cranberry sauce." This statement brought tons of laughter from the group.

Toshi got quiet. "There is something about Jayne."

"You haven't slept with her yet have you?" Raheem asked.

"That is none of your business. It is also not something that is discussed among gentlemen," Toshi said with a very straight face.

All three friends chimed in at the same time. "No, he hasn't!"

"I only met her in October and we are getting to know each other. Like I said, I really like her." His eyes dropped to the table.

Felix said what they all had been thinking, "yeah, but you have got to get through those friends first."

Phở, always the last to add his two *đồng tiềns* said, "I think that Tamika girl scanned my credit cards through my wallet."

Raheem piped up. "Yeah, Phở. She zoomed in on you."

Both Felix and Toshi in unison said, "I ain't saying she's a gold digger….."

As the men finished the verse of the song, Toshi heeded Raheem's words. He had to get through those friends first. It wasn't the friends he was worried about. A larger concern was for Jayne. *Was he a good man?* If what his friends believed and said about him was true, then he needed to be better. He had taken a seat at the playing table and tossed in his chips. He was all in. A woman like Jayne deserved his best and he was going to be a better man. He was going to filter his words and really think about her feelings and what she needed. *I only hope it will be what I need.*

Chapter 12

Jayne fussed and primped all day getting ready for dinner with Toshi. The guest bathroom was double checked three times, the toilet cleaned twice, the special towels hung, and the soap containers refilled. A quick peek under the sink to ensure no personal items were in this bathroom, making certain that everything was okay as she ran the vacuum over the carpet. Still not satisfied, she added some carpet freshener and vacuumed it again. Although she had no plans for him to be in her bedroom, she changed the bed covers, put on the good comforter and the nice pillow shams, before running a dust cloth over all the furniture.

While she was at the market yesterday, she had picked fresh seasonal fruit for the centerpiece on the table. The pound cake had come out of the oven and she was roasting apples with cinnamon to go on the cake. At four o'clock she showered and pressed her clothing. She didn't know why, but she put on a nice set of matching underwear and laughed at herself for taking the extra step. *Nothing is going to happen, but just in case there is a little over the clothes action, I am wearing the good stuff.* It had been a while for Jayne, but she could wait a bit longer. She still wasn't sure about Toshi. Her girlfriends had plenty to say, but this was her time. For whatever reason she and Toshi had been brought together, was yet to be seen.

At five o'clock she removed the apples and put the

parmesan dusted fingerling potatoes in the oven. The table was set with her good dishes and crystal wine glasses. The doorbell rang and Jayne nearly jumped out of her skin. She peeked through the keyhole to find Brionna standing at the door. “Come in,” she told her as she cracked the door.

“Why are you answering the door in your drawers, girl? I thought you were just having him over for dinner?”

“I still have to cook the fish and I don’t want the smell in my clothes.” Brionna looked about the apartment.

“I wanted to see if you needed help with anything?”

Jayne looked about the small two bedroom space. “Nope. I’m good.” *What is this about?*

“Jayne,” she said with the sisterly look. “This guy….” She chewed on her lip a bit as Jayne waited to see what her friend had to say. “He makes you smile, and honestly, you looked good standing next to him.”

“Thanks Bri. Did you come all the way over here to tell me this?”

“No girl. I came to bring you this.” She opened her large purse and removed a love basket, filled with flavored condoms, a penis ring, a vibrating egg, gels, rubs, and some other items that made Jayne blush.

“I don’t need any of that stuff! We are just having dinner and watching the ball drop. Take that freaky shit back to your house!”

“Girl you never know. Those Asian men like this kind of shit.” She headed toward the master bath. “I will just leave this under the sink for future use.”

“No, Brionna! Get out!” She was laughing as she shoved her friend out the door.

At 5:45, she dropped the asparagus in the pot, seared the sea bass, and covered the finished plates with cloches and sat them in the warm oven. The dishes used to cook the meal were washed and put away. She even made Toshi a container to go. At 6:10, he knocked at the door.

Her heart beat sped up as she checked her slacks, patted her hair, and opened the door to welcome him in. She could barely see him behind the gigantic bouquet of flowers.

"Champagne, flowers, and..." He handed her a golden box. "...of course, chocolates." Jayne placed the flowers in a vase and added them to the table. "I hope you are hungry, because dinner is ready."

"It smells delicious. Is that sea bass?"

"Yes." She had not seen him eat anything other than chicken and fish, so she had hoped that the bass was a good choice. "The guest bath is here when you are ready to wash your hands."

Out of habit, Toshi removed his shoes and stepped into the bathroom. One wall was painted orange, adorned with abstract paintings. The shower curtain was an unusual pattern that had matching hand towels. The bathroom even had orange balls of soap and tangerine liquid soap. He was curious and opened the second adjoining door to the bathroom which led into her home office. One wall was painted candy apple red and the other was granny smith green. *What was with the fruit theme?*

It did not take Toshi long before he noticed the sewing machine and the fabric from Joann's. She had gone back to purchase it. Jayne called out to him, "get out of my office Toshi Yamaguchi! Stop being nosey!"

He could not help but laugh, because she had caught him dead to rights. "Get over here so I can feed you this lovely dinner that I have been slaving over all day!"

As he walked to the table, she took him all in. The navy slacks and soft cream colored shirt with a navy zippered sweater with a hood. His cologne was faint, but smelled fresh like an ocean. His hair was a bit spiky on top, with the rest in a ponytail. The goatee that surrounded those luscious lips, had been trimmed since yesterday. Through the sweater, she could see the muscle definition of his arms. As he took his seat, she could see the muscles in his thighs. *Damn, he was fine*! *Covered in sexy and wrapped up in a blanket filled with a mouthful of "oh yeah".*

She removed the cloches from the plates and poured the wine. "Bon appetit."

Toshi eyed the plate and everything looked wonderful. "*Itadakimasu,* Jayne." She strained her mind, remembering the words, "*Dou itashimashite*," as she watched him sink his fork into the bass. It flaked apart. When he put a fork full in his mouth, his eyes rolled up in his head. He moved on to the potatoes, then the asparagus, saying nothing as he cleared the plate. Suddenly, as if he remembered he was not alone, he looked up and started to laugh. "I didn't realize how hungry I was, and it was so delicious, I got lost in the food."

"I will take that as a compliment." The kettle sang as she prepared the water for his tea.

"Jayne," he said as she poured his tea and removed his plate. "You are so talented and warm. Why are you single?"

She kowtowed and served his tea. "Most men don't want what I want. They want what I represent, but not who I am or what I am."

"What would that be?" he asked as he sipped on the perfectly steeped tea.

"Independent, free thinking, and an artist," she told him as she cleared her plate and returned to the table with dessert. He watched her spoon the warm apples over the pound cake, pressing the whipped topping just enough to make the perfect white, sweet flower. The plate of dessert looked restaurant quality. It tasted that way as well.

"Jayne. Can I take a few slices of this cake with me?"

"Of course. I made you a to go plate of everything I cooked tonight."

"Gochisosama," he told her.

Jayne replied, *"Deshita."*

This woman, in Toshi's opinion was incredible. There had to be something wrong, or weird about her that he had yet to spot. "If you keep cooking meals like this, you are going to have a hard time getting rid of me."

"Don't worry. My cousin is a cop and I have pepper spray and a gun." It was said as nonchalantly as if she had just gotten two loaves of bread on sale at the store. He really liked her dry sense of humor.

On the dining room wall was a painting that covered the entire space. Toshi was entranced by the detail and colors of the abstract rendering. When he stood, it was like looking at different painting altogether. He moved to the living room to look at it from far away and was still able to see something he had not spotted earlier. 'This painting is amazing!" He moved closer to examine the brush strokes.

'Thank you," she said shyly.

"You did this?"

"Yes. The one above the couch as well."

The painting above the couch was of a family of four. The sadness in the mother's eyes was haunting. The distance in the father's eyes and expression said something was wrong. The picture depicted the all American family. Even the girl in the pretty pink Sunday dress looked as if her smile had been painted on. Well it had been. He shook his head as he tried to understand everything that Jayne was saying in her brush strokes. She stood beside him and his arm slipped around her waist. He was seeing something special and a view into her inner world. He held his words. She had accused him of having no filters, but his new mission with her was to sift everything that came out of his mouth.

Jane leaned into his strength as his thumb absently rubbed at her hip. His gaze still transfixed on the painting. "Come, Toshi. Have a seat."

He eyed her with a new respect. The art spoke volumes about her private pain. The painting spoke of something unsettled which still resided in her and until it was resolved, there would never be a full-time man in her life. The man in the painting had deserted her and let her down. Toshi silently promised he would not add to her pain.

The remainder of the evening they chatted. She spoke of her job and he talked about his. The subject eased around to dating history and Toshi was honest. He told her that he had been with Ai for nine months, which was probably the longest he had dated anyone.

Jayne confessed that she had been on three disastrous dates since breaking up with George. “My last date was so horrible, that I refused to go out with anyone soon afterward,” she confessed. Toshi snubbed the idea that the dates had been *that* bad until Jayne told him about Phillip.

“The evening started out fine.” She told him about dinner at his place with some Chinese takeout. He had chosen a movie that she wanted to see, but when Phillip was informed about how she liked to Cosplay, he took it to mean something else. “He excused himself to get more comfortable and I understood. He was still in a tie from work.” Toshi asked if he came back in draw string pants and his shirt opened to the waist.

“That would have been an improvement over what he came back wearing, Toshi.” She sipped at her wine. “That fool walked out of his bedroom in a leopard Zentai suit with the crotch missing! His junk was on the ready and it was pointing at me, like it was saying, “you’re next”!”

The visual that formed in Toshi’s mind, made him burst into laughter. “He told me that he liked to play dress up too. He said this through the zipper that covered his mouth, as he started prancing about the room, like he was stalking his prey. He even froze in the middle of the floor and licked at his knuckles like some big old special needs patient who thought he was a cat!” This caused Toshi to fall over on the couch in gut busting guffaws.

Toshi was choking because he was laughing so hard.

When he was able to speak, he said, "what did you do Jayne?"

"I told him to hang on. I have my suit in the car. Let me go grab it and we can play together."

Toshi was still chuckling, mainly at the expression on her face. She was scowling like she had smelled something horrible. "Did you come back Jayne?"

"Hell no! I got in my car and drove my happy ass home!" Toshi laughed harder. "I saw that jackass last week in Macy's, He spotted me and tried to dart out of my way so I wouldn't see him. He ran into the pillar, nearly knocking his silly butt out." Toshi was holding his stomach asking her to stop. He was worried he was going to lose his dinner from laughing so hard.

"It's not funny Toshi. When men find out I like to draw comics and Cosplay, they automatically think I like to dress up and play kinky sex games."

"I wondered as much myself, especially when I saw that basket under the bathroom sink."

Jayne gasped. "I can't believe Brionna left that shit here! And why are you snooping under my sink?" She jumped up and ran to the bathroom, grabbing the basket and throwing the items in the trash. This only made him laugh harder. It took almost an hour for him to stop cracking a smile every time he looked at her.

The time had sped by. It was 11:55. Where had six hours gone? He was still chuckling as she gathered the champagne glasses and handed him the bottle. She turned on the television to see Ryan Seacrest prepping the crowd. Jayne handed him his coat, grabbed her pistol from the closet, and drug him out to the balcony. Toshi's eyes were glued to the gun. She *really* had a gun!

The countdown began. At the stroke of midnight Toshi popped the cork, poured them both a glass, and watched Jayne shoot into the wood line. "Would you like to shoot it as well?"

He shook his head no and handed her the glass. Jayne intertwined her left arm into his like a wedding toast with the right hand still holding the revolver. "Happy New year Toshi!"

"Happy New Year Jayne," he said as he lowered his head and kissed her tenderly.

He placed his free hand on her waist and was careful not to stand too close. He deepened the kiss just a bit and then pulled away. She was still holding a gun.

"Thank you for a wonderful evening Jayne. Is there anything I can do to help you clean up?" He rinsed the glasses and collected the bag of his to go plates.

Disappointment covered her face. *What had you expected? You are still holding a gun.*

Toshi saw the look on her face, allowing his eyes to trail to the gun. She sat down the weapon. He used both hands to pull her in close, pressing her back to the fridge. He laid one on her that made her right leg shake like a dog having his belly stroked. She accidently pressed the ice dispenser, causing ice cubes to shoot everywhere.

"Good night Jayne," he said as he released her to let himself out of the front door with his to go plates in hand. "Call me."

Toshi was grinning as he walked away.

Yep. He is using a new tactic. Unfortunately for Jayne, this one was working much better. She even liked the new approach. He just upped the ante. Her next move was going to cost a few more chips.

Chapter 13

The grinning had not stopped when he went by his parent's home on Thursday. The lawn care company hadn't done a very good job and the gutters were brimming over with pine straw. He parked his car, using his house keys to let himself in the back door. His old bedroom hadn't changed very much and spare sets of clothing were still in the closet. Toshi made a quick change into a long sleeved work shirt, a pair of faded sweats, and some old sneaks, then he put his ear buds in his ears and headed to the shed. Gloved up and on a ladder, he started on the far corner and worked his way toward the back door, singing along with tunes from his iPod.

Hirishito Yamaguchi arrived home after a grueling day of irrelevant meetings which had accomplished nothing more than increase his desire to retire. It angered him that the staff wanted to corporatize his operation. They suggested that he place tablets on each Hibachi station so that the patrons could place their orders. Bah! The pleasure of dining at a Japanese steakhouse is the experience, the togetherness, and the joy of watching fresh food being prepared before you. His operations manager also wanted to cut food costs by buying pre-made sauces and precut vegetables. Hirishito's was built on his blood, sweat, and precise knife cuts. He nearly fired the punk on the spot. A sigh escaped his lips as he shuffled through the front door on legs with broken veins and swollen knees. He suffered pains of the trade of a chef, who stood on his feet for too many hours a day. He would soon retire. Soon Kunio would be finished with medical school, married and starting a family of her own. Then he could sell the whole chain, move to Florida, and spend weekends with his grandchildren. Another sigh escaped tired lips. Kunio would be their only hope. He wasn't sure what was going on with his son.

As he entered the kitchen, he heard an odd sound as his wife and daughter stared out the kitchen window. "Eri," he asked. "What is that dreadful sound?"

Kunio answered, "It is Toshi. *Otousan,* he is singing."

"And cleaning out the gutters," Eri added.

Hirishito stepped up to the window and stared out as well. His son was singing and dancing in a way that was not proper with women watching, or for cleaning out the gutters! At the age of sixteen, Toshi had used his allowance to pay his friends to clean out the gutters. Even when he started his job at the university, he hired a lawn care company to come by and handle the yard work. Hirishito was shocked to see him on the ladder.

"What is all of this about, Eri?" he asked his wife.

"I don't know, but he looks..." she paused, exhaling in disbelief. "...happy."

On cue, Toshi turned and spotted his family in the window. He gave them an ear to ear grin and waved. All three onlookers shrank back as if watching a 3-D movie with an axe flying at their faces. In between bagging damp pine straw, he would stop, freestyle dance, then get back to the task at hand.

Eri understood what was going on and did not hesitate to speak her mind. "He is having weird sex with the black woman."

Kunio shook her head. "I don't think so *Okaachan*. If they have, it was recent, because last week she averted her eyes when he came out of his room partially dressed. I don't think she has seen him naked."

Hirishito was shocked at the conversation between his wife and daughter. "Kunio! You have met this woman that Toshi is seeing?"

"I have, *Otousan*. She is nice, pretty, and he really likes her. She makes him smile."

Hirishito tried not to be prideful at the cordiality and warmth of his wife and daughter. Toshi was completely the opposite. He trusted few, spoke to even less, and rarely cracked a smile. In elementary school, the principal wanted him tested to make sure he wasn't suffering with a form of Autism. The battery of tests proved the opposite. His son had an extremely high I.Q.

When Hirishito enrolled him in martial arts classes, he would win tournaments because his unwavering gaze intimidated the other opponents, resulting in forfeitures. He and Eri spent many nights worrying if he would ever be successful or find a wife, since he went through women like wine. He was bored of them after only a few months. Even when he broke his wrist and had to leave medical school, his face registered no emotion. Toshi shifted his focus and trudged on, never discussing the issue with any of them. There were still days when, as his parents, they felt they did not know their own son. Hirishito looked out the window again, just to be certain of what he had seen.

He was still singing and dancing. Eri opened the back door. "Toshi, are you staying for dinner?"

"I would love to! *Haha*! Are you making my favorites?" He flashed her a wide grin.

Eri nodded and closed the back door, then looked at her husband. "What are his favorites?" She then burst into tears. Her son was 30 years old and she did not know what he liked to eat, because anything you put in front of him, he would devour.

Hirishito took her in his arms. "Whatever you cook will be fine." One thing was certain. They had to meet this woman in Toshi's life.

Chapter 14

“Grammy, it’s me!” Jayne called out as she entered the front door of her family home. The pound cake she had baked for dinner the other day was taunting her and she felt it best if it found a new home. Grandpa Joe loved her pound cake, mainly because she only made it on special occasions. When Grandma Pearl saw the cake, she went into the closet and started praying.

Jayne knew better than be disrespectful and interrupt a woman conversing with the Man upstairs, but she wasn’t certain what had inspired the sudden need to open the line of communication. She refused to eavesdrop and set about slicing a piece of cake for Grandpa Joe to go with his afternoon cup of decaf. She even heated the apples adding a smidgen of the whipped cream.

Her grandfather was not really a man who watched television with the exception of an UGA football game or some really good fly fishing. This evening he was watching Duck Dynasty and laughing like it was the funniest thing he had ever seen. “Grandpa?” she asked. “What has Grammy so upset that she is praying? If you don’t mind me asking.”

Grandpa took a big slice of cake and shoved it between his bushy mustache and grey beard. Somewhere, in betwixt the scraggly hair resided his lips and mouth. “Chile, she’s praying for you!”

Jayne’s eyebrows shot up. “Me? What did I do?”

Grandpa waited for the commercial before answering. “It is not what you have done, but what you are thinking about doing girl."

She closed her eyes, saying a silent prayer herself. "What is it she believes I am about to do Grandpa Joe?"

This question caused a roar of laughter from the old man. "She thinks you are about to do the young man you cooked this cake for, Chile." He started to laugh again.

Grandma Pearl knew a great deal, but she didn't know everything. Jayne wasn't sure how she felt about Toshi yet, although she did like kissing him. Sleeping with him hadn't entered her mind. She understood that her Grammy worried about her and men, especially considering what had happened with Jayne's mom, but she and Lillie Mae Carter Wright were two different women.

Lillie had also been a different woman before she met and fell in love with Malik Terrell Wright. The newlyweds had been inseparable and madly in love which led to the birth of their first child. A boy named Darnell. A year later, a girl child was stillborn, which began Lillie's concern for their fitness as parents. It helped very little that each time the couple came to visit her parents, her mother would leave the room and spend thirty minutes in the closet in prayer. Grandma Pearl did not like Lillie's husband and felt the man had a wandering eye and a lustful heart. There must have been some truth to what Grammy believed, because a few months later, Lillie came home from work to find Malik in his tool shed with the neighbor, Shanice Longmire. She was playing with his tool.

Lillie forgave him, while blaming it on the loss of the daughter. The constant illness of little Darnell, was putting a strain on their relationship. Six months later, Lillie found herself pregnant with little Jayne, who was born the following summer, weighing in at seven pounds six ounces. The little bundle of joy caused friction between the couple, because Lillie had given the girl a *white* first name and Malik gave her the *black* middle name of LaQueeda. This was the one thing that Grandma Pearl agreed with Malik on. Heck it was the only thing she agreed with him on. Once Pearlie Jean Carter made up her mind on something, there was no turning back, no changing it, and no convincing her otherwise. Lillie had given up listening to what she considered nonsense from her mother and set about living her life and raising her family. If Malik was unfaithful, she saw no signs of it. Grandma Pearl told her she couldn't see the signs no more than an ostrich could see the hyenas coming up on it with its head stuck in the ground and his ass tooted in the air.

Lillie's head came out the sand when Malik was supposed to be watching his children. Five year old Darnell left through the front door and wandered into the streets. The driver never saw the child chasing the ball. Darnell was killed on impact. Darnell had brittle bones, digestive issues, and underdeveloped lungs which made him far smaller than your average five year old. It also hastened his arrival to the pearly gates.

It was the sirens and ambulance that brought Malik out of the shed with the neighboring women, Molly Cartwright and Imani Jackson. The irony in the whole mess was that Shanice Longmire was the one who heard Jayne's cries and came out to investigate. Lillie came home to find her husband being comforted by the two women he had been with and a deceased son. What made it worse in her eyes, was that her husband was not even holding his own daughter.

Lillie never recovered and Grandma Pearl would not let her live it down. Since Pearlie Jean seemed to know what was best for everybody, Lillie packed up Jayne's meager belongings and took them to her mother. She handed Pearlie Jean the custody papers and the bag of diapers along with a wide eyed Jayne. Lillie climbed into her car and drove to Gwinnett County, far away from her mother's prayer circle and checked into the Summitt Ridge Mental Health Center where she stayed for four years.

Malik sent a monthly check to Grandma Pearl for Jayne's needs, but Pearlie Jean put it in a savings account. When Jayne graduated from high school, her college fund was fat, full, and ready to support her four years at the University of Georgia. Jayne had earned a few scholarships as well, so the Darnell Wright fund also paid for graduate school.

Jayne rarely spoke to her father. He never remarried, because Lillie would never grant him a divorce on the grounds of her mental instability. He sent birthday and Christmas presents, but stopped calling when she was about 12 years old. Ironically, he also sent her the first set of acrylic paints and brushes. Infidelity had cost him his family and his need to play with the neighborhood women, had cost him his son's life.

He was never truly a part of Jayne's life and it was fine by Jayne. Grandpa Joe had been a much better father and Grandma Pearl had become less crazy in her religious zeal, especially after Lillie told her all her praying didn't save her grandson.

Grandma Pearl had finished her conversation with the Almighty and she joined Jayne and Grandpa Joe in the living room with a slice of cake and apples. It only took her two bites before she said, "before it goes any further, we want to meet this young man."

"Grammy. He and I are just friends. He came over for dinner on New Year's Eve and I cooked for him. That's all."

"Chile, who you think you fooling? You were with the water headed fella George for nearly a year and you never made him your pound cake," Grandma Pearl said with a touch of sarcasm.

Grandpa Joe interjected, "she got a point there Girl!"

"Grammy!" Jayne struggled to find the right phrasing, but in looking for the correct word in one sentence, she said the incorrect one in the second sentence. "Grammy, he cooked dinner for me on Christmas Eve. I returned the courtesy and cooked dinner for Toshi the week after."

Grandpa Joe sat up in the recliner, lowering the leg rest, and jumping up in one motion. Grandma Pearl sat her cake down before she pretended to faint and fall to the floor. Grandpa tried to get Pearlie Jean off the floor while at the same time, grabbing at his heart, Fred Sanford style, bellowing, "we are being invaded by the Japanese again, Pearlie Jean!"

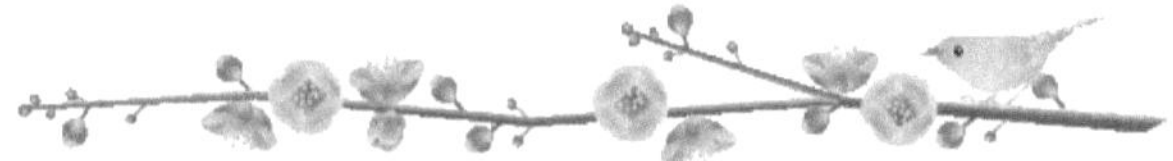

The smelling salts were retrieved from the first aid kit

to be waived under Grandma Pearl's nose. Jayne knew the woman hadn't actually passed out, but it made her feel better to stick the pungent bag under her nose to get her up off of the floor. Once up righted in her Queen Anne chair, Grandpa Joe fussed over his wife a bit, then gave Jayne the stink eye.

"Toshi and I are just friends. Nothing more." She tried to comfort her grandparents.

Grandpa Joe was the first to speak. "Chile, men of other races may date you, but they won't marry you."

"Men of my own race aren't marrying me either," Jayne blurted out.

"Don't sass your Grandpa, girl!" She received the reprimand from her grandmother and disliked the taste it left in her mouth. Jayne decided she wasn't going to swallow what these two were trying to feed her.

She sat on the ottoman, leaning forward to touch both of their hands. "Dating has changed so much in the last ten years and finding a good man is difficult." Jayne went on to explain to her grandparents that there were more black men in prison today than there were in slavery in 1850. Grandpa Joe gasped. She wasn't done hitting them with some other cold hard facts. "The black men who are free are either gay, pretending to not be gay, or so bullheaded you can't stand to be around them for more than fifteen minutes at a time."

"There are still some good black men out there, Chile. I know of several in my church," Grandma Pearl insisted.

Jayne countered her argument. "They are in church to prey on those women who go to church to find a man. More than likely Grammy, those same men are having relations with at least two to three women in your church." Grandma Pearl's hand flew to her ample bosom as if she were completely in disbelief.

Grandpa Joe was nodding his head because he knew it was true. "Grammy, a decent brother knows he has his pick and is often shared with more than one woman. You see it all the time on these reality shows. Women fighting over a scrap of man." She repeated the mantra that her Grandma had taught her, about having a piece of man.

"Chile, if you are ready for a good man, then you should get on your knees and ask the Good Lord to send you one." Which was her grandmother's fall back answer to everything. Jayne was about to out maneuver the old bible thumper.

"I did Grammy," she told her as she looked from her grandpa's face to her grandmother's. "And Toshi showed up. I am moving slowly, taking my time, but as I said, we are just friends."

She knew Grandma Pearl would not have a comeback for that one.

Chapter 15

On a quiet Friday night at home alone, again, Jayne began to give some real thought about the men she had come across in the past six months. Had she missed a potential gem in the bag of Fruit Loops? Using a scrap of paper, she listed all the men who had asked her out since her breakup with George. Phillip was crossed off the list immediately. Ricky had dated Brionna. Rodrick was still married although he swore they were separated, but living under the same roof. Benjamin was nice, had a warm smile, and six children by six different women. Then there was LaDell, who worked in her building. She even had his number.

She picked up her phone to place the call, but it started to vibrate in her hand. She turned it over to see Toshi's face. It was the stupid picture he had taken in Atlanta. "Hey you!"

"You busy tomorrow?"

"Thank you for asking Toshi. I am fine. How goes your day?" He chuffed in the phone and picked up on her dig.

"Sorry," he paused. "How are you Jayne?"

She repeated her statement. "Thank you for asking Toshi. I am fine. How goes your day?"

"Very well, thank you for asking," he responded as he smiled. "I was wondering, Jayne. Are you busy tomorrow around lunch time?"

"I am not, but I do have some plans later in the evening, why what's up?"

"I wanted to run down to Hancock Fabrics, look at

some patterns, and get your feedback on a few things. Oh yeah, and I will buy you lunch."

"Sounds good. You want me to drive, since you are buying?"

"Nope. I will pick you up at 11:30."

"Okay, sounds good," she told him as she hung up the phone. For some odd reason she turned into a pure girl and ran to check her closet to find something to wear.

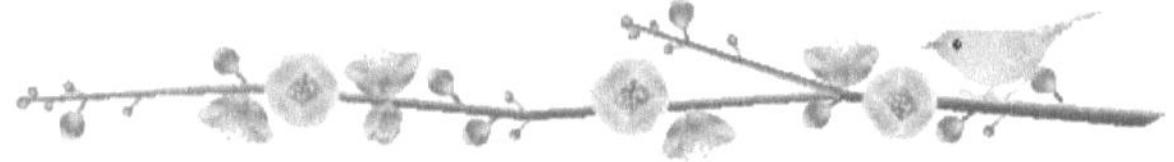

Jayne was ready at 11 am, dressed in grey slacks, a pink cardigan set, and her lightweight grey pea coat. The pearls that were given to her as a graduation present by her Grammy, were the only real pieces of jewelry she wore outside of a pair of earring studs and her watch. She thought Toshi would text her when he arrived, but was pleasantly surprised when he came to the door.

He was a gentleman as he opened the door for her. Once inside the car, she noticed how clean everything was. Not even a speck of dust on the dashboard. The faint scent of his soap lingered in the car. As he rounded the front of the car, she checked the floors for wrappers of any kind. Nothing. "I know a great place to grab a bite after we hit the store. Or do you want to eat first?"

Jayne noticed that he turned down the music before starting the car. "Hancock's." She eyed him suspiciously. "But first tell me what's on your iPod."

"What do you mean?" he asked as he pulled away from the parking space to exit the complex.

"You turned down the music. What is in the cd player? Is it something horribly embarrassing like The Back

Street Boys or N' Sync?" She laughed as she reached for the volume knob, "Or worse…Miley Cyrus!"

As she turned up the music, she found it was Barry White, crooning *Practice What Your Preach*. "That is not what I expected," she said with wide eyes.

"I'm an old school kind of guy. I love songs that have a story and a meaning, like this one."

"What kind of story, Toshi? He is horny and asking her to come over and back up what she has been saying to him," Jayne said with a flippant attitude.

He shook his head explaining that the woman in the song was probably some smart ass, who is making promises which she has yet to keep. "He knows she is lying, but he makes sure she understands that when they do finally get together, he is going to teach her a thing a two about how to treat a man."

Almost in unison with the song, Jayne says, "Really?"

Toshi began to sing along with the song, he looks over at her, and begins to sing the words to her. Jayne finished the lyrics the lyric in the sentence. They continued the ride down Washington Road, singing the song and going back and forth until they had arrived at Hancock's. Toshi pulled into the parking lot with a wide grin on his face. He really liked Jayne. Out of all the women he had dated, she was the first to get it. She was also the only to sing along with him, although he was not a singer.

This was going to be a fun afternoon.

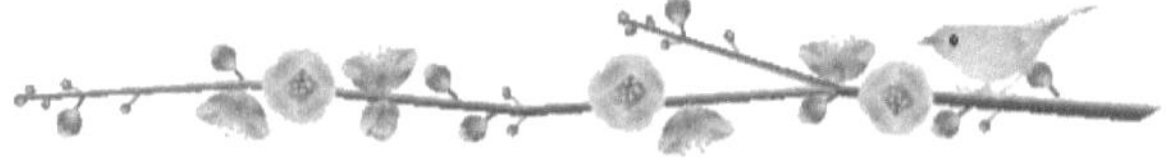

An hour was spent in the fabric store, looking at fabrics and patterns. She made some suggestion to altering some of the patterns, but in the end, suggested he would come out better making his own. They talked about conferences, with Jayne admitting that she was not planning to attend SacAnime, but maybe one large and two smaller conferences later in the year. "The one I truly want to go to is the Anime Expo in Los Angeles in July."

"I have thought about going to that one as well, but it's so large, you can get lost there," he told her as he pulled into Yosko. "I am in the mood for some sushi."

"I have never eaten here before. I take it the food is good if you like it."

Toshi liked her confidence in him, which continued through lunch as she trusted him to order for her. He ordered vegetables, rice, and a Sierra roll for her. He ordered something she could not pronounce for himself. Jayne opened the conversation about him.

Toshi was forthcoming with his wish to start a comic book, create unique characters, and have a booth at a con.

"Do it," she told him as she nibbled at salad drenched in way too much ginger dressing.

"Just like that? Start a comic book?"

"Sure, there is a ton of software that makes it easy. Kindle also has a format to get in the Amazon online store. You can even get started by launching a web comic first, but you know all this already. Why are your dragging your feet on your dream?"

It was said out loud. The food arrived but Toshi sat staring at her, "Why haven't you?"

Jayne blessed the food and sampled a piece of the Sierra roll. "This is really good." She took another piece, but he was still waiting. "I am great with writing and color schemes, but drawing the characters? As you saw, I need some work."

He nibbled at his fingernail, then took a bite of his sushi roll. "I guess I am kind of scared. You know, you put it out there and people hate it."

"Tell me about the concept," she said as she gobbled down the sushi.

Toshi lowered his voice to a whisper. The story, as he told it, revolved around a man who had received super powers from aliens who visited earth, called *The Others*. The main character used his powers to clean up crime in the neighborhood, but the local drug czar took it out on the community, killing the hero's family and turning him into a vigilante.

"Cool!" She told him. "Let's do it!"

He stopped chewing, not understanding her suggestion. "Do what?"

"Let's create a comic book, web comic, and super hero team!" She slapped her hands on the table. "I want to be a character too. I want to be a vigilante as well." She said it like a school kid who wanted to try out as the soccer team's mascot.

"Just like that?" He snapped his fingers.

"Yeah," she told him. "Why not? Between the two of us, we have everything we need to start our own comic book."

He was shaking his head no while she was nodding her head yes. "I can do the whole marketing campaign and build the website. We will launch it a few pages at a time to build a following in February."

Toshi was still shaking his head no. Jayne was

nonplussed. "It is January. We have until July to get the actual comics in print and debut it at the AnimeExpo, but we need to get a booth now!"

He was still shaking his head no. Jayne kept moving forward. "My cousin is a lawyer and she can draw up a contract for us. We can call our company..." She paused looking for the right words. "Oooh, Ooh, ooh! I know!" She smiled a gigantic grin with seaweed in her teeth. On the table she did a mock drum roll. "We call it ToJay!"

He was still shaking his head no. Jayne forged ahead. "Okay fine. JayTos Comics. Yeah, I like that much better."

"Jayne, it takes money to start a business, funding, and so much more," he told her trying to dampen her enthusiasm.

"Oh, Booo!" she said as she ate her final piece of sushi. "My cousin started a business for $1500 dollars and makes good money selling trashy eBooks on Kindle."

Toshi was frowning. "How many cousins do you have Jayne?"

"Lots. I am throwing down the gauntlet Toshi! Are you in or do you want to keep pining about it and talking about what you want to do? Or are you ready to grab that nasty ole' bull by its cajones and ride it all the way to the finish line?"

Toshi leaned back in the chair, listening, thinking, and plotting. It could be done. They could actually do this. "I can do the drawings, but the writing am not so strong on. With back ground coloring I tend to go dark."

"I am always bright and colorful which will bring a nice balance to the panels." She was still grinning.

Having sipped some of the water, the seaweed had been washed from her teeth.

"Are you serious Jayne? You really want to do this with me?"

"I am as serious as sin or my name isn't Jayne LaQueeda Wright."

Toshi furrowed his eyebrows. "Your middle name is LaQueeda?"

"Yes Toshi. It is. Now focus. I will be your partner and we will create a comic book together." She was smiling at him again. "What is your middle name?"

He sat for another moment, gathering his thoughts. "I don't have one." He paused again. "Okay, let's do it. Where do we start?"

Jayne dug into her bag and pulled out a journal, ripping out two sheets, giving one to him. "First we brainstorm, then divide the research duties." She scribbled as she went along. Toshi sat watching the birth of the comic company come alive on bits of torn out notebook paper.

Jayne LaQueeda Wright was about to change his life.

Chapter 16

Each Saturday evening, Jayne and Toshi had been meeting to hash out design concepts and details. The initial sketches of the vigilantes were drawn in charcoal, which highlighted some of the major strengths of each character. Jayne was not quite pleased with Toshi's drawing of her character, so the following weekend, she brought over her own rendition. He wasn't pleased with hers either at this point. The only thing they were agreeing upon was the font for the cover of the comic. Hence, they had reached a stalemate which led to Jayne suggesting they step away from the process for a minute to get some perspective.

On the second Saturday in February, instead of meeting with her new pal, Jayne decided to join her friends for lunch. Brionna was the first to notice Jayne's distraction, but it was RaShunda who made the comments. "Girl, I don't know why you're wasting your time on that man. It's not going to go anywhere."

This was followed by Tamika's sarcasm. "I know you aren't trying to sleep with him. You are only going to be hungry an hour later anyway." This comment garnered snickers from the other two, but Jayne remained quiet. Her mind was on a marketing concept. She had been given a big assignment at work which was taking most of her energy and the Saturday nights with Toshi were tapping into her reserves of calm and tolerance. By the time Sunday rolled around for church and dinner with her grandparents, she was completely worn out.

Brionna touched her hand. "Jayne, we want you to be happy, but we are just advising that before you pack your bags and climb aboard the Orient Express, you may want to get back out there first."

By the end of lunch, Jayne was ready to wash her hands of Toshi, the comic book, and her meddlesome, bitchy ass friends. Tonight was a free night and she was going home to soak, put on some jazz, light some candles around the tub, and down a bottle of Chenin Blanc. Jayne was well aware that she would never hear the end of it, but she had made the mental commitment to forego church in the morning as well. Brionna was half right. She had to gain some perspective.

Jayne grabbed her purse, took out thirty dollars and laid it on the table. She gave her friends a mock salute and headed for the door with them calling after her. *Make the bad women shut up*. "I'll call you guys later," she chirped over her shoulder. When she turned around, Jayne had come into contact with something very large, very solid and smelled like a night of being face down biting on a pillow.

"Well, if it isn't Jayne Wright," a deep tenor voice said to the top of her head. Jayne looked up to see LaDell Richardson with his large hands on her arms.

"LaDell, I was thinking about you last week." Which was the truth, but she did not admit that she had almost called him.

"Can you think about me next Friday when I take you out to dinner?"

Over her shoulder, she could hear her girlfriends answering for her. In her mind, it was too much of a coincidence to let it pass.

"Sure. Why not?" He suggested they meet after work at the front door of the building they both worked in.

"How does Italian sound?"

"One of my favorites," she mumbled as she tried to get away from him. "Does six o' clock sound okay to you?"

Just like that, she had a date for next Friday. It wasn't until she returned home and jotted it on her calendar, that she realized it was Valentine's Day.

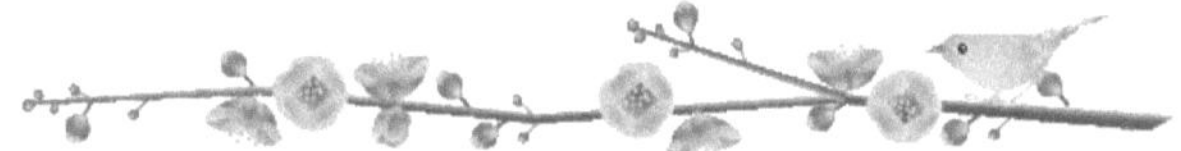

It was a simple black dress, with a mint green cashmere cardigan, her pearls and a pair of black and green sling backs with a kitten heel. Everyone in the office acted as if she had come to work dressed for the prom. At six on the dot, she grabbed her coat and headed down to the main lobby. When she exited the elevator on the left, LaDell was coming down the stairs on the right.

He was a gentleman and helped her with her coat, telling her she looked wonderful and smelled fantastic. "I will drive. I'll just bring you back here to get your car." He chuckled at a joke that she didn't find humorous. "I mean, if anything weird happens, you know where I work."

She wished she had brought her gun. By the end of the evening, something was destined to die. Jayne reprimanded herself for being negative before the date even started. Her fists were clenched, but she quickly released them, convincing herself it was going to be a great evening.

It wasn't.

Before they left the building, at least eight women had called his name. Three gave those high school, *I have a crush on you* finger waves. Two others blew him a kiss. One rubbed her breasts while mouthing *call me* and the final three gave him the stink eye. Grandma Pearl always said, if you want to know the habits of an animal, observe it in its natural environment. LaDell was a lion who used the office building as a hunting ground.

Yet, Jayne did not want to pass judgment on him based on a few friendly women. He was, by any woman's standards, a very attractive man. LaDell easily stood a bit over six feet, was solidly built, without an ounce of fat on him. He had a low haircut, a perfectly groomed goatee, and a nice smile with really big teeth. His skin tone was a smooth, rich, creamy peanut butter beige, with jet black hair and deep brown eyes. The brother also has some really big feet and hands. All of this matched perfectly to his very big, black, and shiny BMW 740i. The front license plate read, "Engineers Do It with Precision."

It put Jayne off a bit, especially when his windshield held four business cards and a scented note. Women could be overly aggressive sometimes, which Jayne understood. It made her feel a bit more at ease when he removed the items and tossed them in the trash. They both laughed as he removed the pair of underwear that someone had tied to his side mirror. From the looks of the red lacy fabric, they were damp.

"Where are we headed for dinner LaDell?" Jayne asked with a smile on her face. He grinned back at her. "I thought Augustino's would be nice," he said as he pressed the fob to unlock the vehicle.

"Great," she told him, still smiling. "I will meet you there!" She turned around and headed to her car. He called after her, but she was not getting into the sex machine with him and she sure as hell was not going to be seen leaving the parking lot in it. Guilt by association held a lot of people in prison, which would also describe how she felt during dinner.

He ordered a $70 dollar bottle of wine to start the meal. A hearty Bordeaux. She explained that the heavy tannins in the wine gave her a hangover, yet he insisted that she at least give it a taste. It was good wine, but an absolute waste, since she barely sipped at the glass she had. The wait staff knew LaDell by name and quickly asked if he desired the Ossobuco as his meal selection. He opted instead for a very large steak with potatoes, while Jayne chose a seafood dish on a bed of pasta with greens.

None of it was enjoyed. Over appetizers, he took out his phone to show her all the projects he had designed accompanied by images of his two awards, along with an accidental peek at a photo in his phone of a woman loving him with her mouth. As she picked at her shrimp, the conversation continued about the wide world of LaDell focusing on the other things he had achieved. Jayne knew she was supposed to be impressed, but only a faint smile could be mustered when the dozen of roses came to the table. A beautiful dessert for two arrived over his conversation about what LaDell had in mind for his new year.

"I'm ready to settle down Jayne. I am looking for that

right woman." He eyed her with earnest. Jayne had been making circles in the chocolate and whipped cream on the plate, not even realizing he had been talking to her.

"Did you hear me Jayne?"

This must have been the point in the evening where his dates would swoon and the panties would dampen. It wasn't happening for her though. She was totally bored by the whole scenario, but she felt cheeky and thought she would play along.

"I was thinking the same thing, LaDell. I am ready too!"

His eyes were wide, thinking he was closing the deal, but Jayne had a plan to shut him down. "I checked my ovulation calendar and tonight is the night, LaDell. I am so ready." Her hand reached across the table to caress his. "I can't wait for you to take me in your arms and make me yours while giving me your seed."

LaDell had started to draw back his hand, looking as if he had been told that she had a yeast infection. Jayne was not going to let him off the hook that easy. She rose from her chair and walked around the table. His eyes were wide again as he watched her approached him, pushing the table to give her enough room to plop down in his lap.

"The answer is yes LaDell. Yes! Yes, I will make you the happiest man in the world and marry you!"

The restaurant erupted in applause. LaDell started to sputter, choking as he tried to hammer out words to tell her she had misunderstood him. Jayne rubbed his face as she gave him a *I am going to tear that up tonight* look, whispering in his ear, "pay that damned check so we can get out of here and get our family started." Still having trouble finding his words, Jayne commenced to patting his pockets to find his wallet. She knew it was in his sport coat's front jacket pocket. She still used the opportunity to run her hands over him, wagging her finger at him as she came close to touching little LaDell.

Wallet found, she went through it looking for the right credit card, waving it in the air at the waiter. "Hurry up and settle our check! We have some celebrating to do!" Jayne added some flair from her Misty Knight impersonation, chipping in a sister girl neck roll complete with pursed lips.

By the time the waiter had returned, the bottle of wine had been recorked and stuffed in her purse, while egging him to get his coat on. The roses were hoisted into her left arm, while chatting away at him. "I knew you were the right one LaDell. I just knew today was going to be my lucky day."

He signed the $200 dinner tab, as she pulled him by the hand. "Wish us luck everyone!" She yelled to the crowded restaurant as a dazed and utterly confused LaDell followed along behind her with the people clapping and shouting well wishes. His eyes were darting back and forth when they reached the parking lot.

"Jayne, I...." He started to stutter.

A calm hand was placed in the center of his chest. "LaDell. We are not all the same. Your fancy car, expensive wine, and accomplishments mean nothing to a woman who has achieved a great deal as well."

He lowered his head as if he were ashamed. "Thank you for dinner. Have a good evening."

"Jayne," he called after her. "I am so sorry."

She walked back over to him lowering her voice. "So am I." She was not one prone to lying, but in this case he deserved it. She channeled Misty Knight again. "I was soooo going to sleep with you tonight! I haven't had any in almost a year too! Oohh and I was going to ride your big ass until my back gave out!"

She sighed. "Oh well!"

Through her rearview mirror she saw him lean against his car, wondering what had just happened.

In the corner of the restaurant, a friend pulled out his phone to make a call. It was answered on the third ring. "Dude, I am in Augustino's and I just saw your girl. I think she just agreed to marry some big black dude."

"Wait, start from the top," Toshi said as he sat and listened to Felix recap everything that had transpired. When he hung up the phone, he eyed the little grey felt box from Kay Jewelers which held the Valentine's present he had bought for Jayne. He was not a drinking man. The strongest thing he had in his apartment was a bottle of Sake. A half drank bottle. Toshi had some things he needed to get off his chest. It had started to rain which further darkened his mood. An hour later, the bottle was nearly empty but Toshi Yamaguchi was up to his neck in emotions.

"Who does she think she is anyway?" he asked himself.

Twenty minutes later, in the down pour of rain, he put the box in his pocket and began to stumble his way to her building. He took a short cut through the tennis courts, around the guest house, and over the hill, finding himself at her doorstep.

He banged on the door, calling her name. “Jayne LaQueeda Wright! You open this damned door right now!”

Chapter 17

The man was soaked from head to toe, rain droplets hanging from the strands of his hair, and he looked absolutely adorable to Jayne. At least he did until his opened his mouth, exhaling 32 proof breath fueled with liquid courage and a jealous temper tantrum.

"Is he in there Jayne?"

"Is who in where?"

Toshi was teetering from side to side. "You know who Jayne. Your new fiancé!" She had no idea what he was talking about, but in those wet clothes he was going to catch a serious cold.

"Toshi, let's talk inside," she told him. She reached for him to pull him across the threshold. Toshi snatched his arm away like a kid on the playground in a game of keep away.

"If he is in there Jayne, I going to kick him in his dick!" Jayne tried to grab him again, but he skirted away from her, bending down with his hands on his knees, getting louder with every word. "He can't make love to you Jayne with a broke dick! I am going to break his dick Jayne!" Toshi began making karate chops in the air while simulating groin kicks, supplemented with Bruce Lee sounds.

Ms. Betty, her neighbor opened her door. "Jayne, is everything okay out there?"

She ran out of her apartment while grabbing Toshi by the arm. "Yes ma'am. Everything is fine."

"You sure? I got the po-po on speed dial!" She had her

fingers on her medical alert necklace. Jayne held up her hand to hold her off. “I got him Ms. Betty. You can go back inside.”

It was a struggle to get a drunken 160 pound man into her apartment, especially with him being uncooperative, yelling, and threatening to open a can of Japanese dick kicking. He clearly outweighed her by 45 pounds, but she needed to get him out of those wet clothes. He kicked off his own shoes when he stepped inside the door and removed his wet jacket letting it flop to the floor.

“I’ve been working on my filters Jayne, working hard too. Look what it got me!” He stood still as she pulled the wet shirt up and over his head, rubbing his skin briskly with one of the towels she had taken from the guest bathroom to warm up his cold skin. “I have been working on being a better man for you too Jayne.” As he rambled on about filters and his quest to be better, Jayne’s focus was on how she was going to get off those wet pants.

The towel was draped about his shoulders. “How much have you had to drink Toshi?”

“I don’t drink,” he said through hiccups.

“What did you sip on tonight then,” she asked while going into the bathroom to retrieve a larger bath towel. Maybe if she held up the towel, he could remove pants allowing her to wrap the material about his waist.

“I had a little bit of Sake. That’s all.” This was said as he tried to stand still, while weaving from side to side.

Jayne opened the towel wide, covering him from the waist down, while asking him to remove his pants. “How much is a little?”

He laughed as the pants dropped down around his

ankles. "The whole damn bottle, Jayne. The whole bottle!" He plopped down on the futon in her office with his bottom lip poked out. "I was trying to wash down the feelings."

Before Jayne went any further, she heeded her Grammy's words, *a man full of the Devil's brew, will tell the truth on him and you.* Something was definitely wrong, because Toshi normally treated his body like a temple and was not one for drinking anything stronger than wine or tea. The man didn't even drink soda. If he downed a whole bottle of Sake, then something heavy was weighing him down. If she was going to get some answers, now would be the best time. 'Toshi, what feelings were you trying to drown?"

He raised his hand as if he were the first one to solve the tough math problem the teacher had placed on the board. "That's the word, drown. I was trying to drown these feelings Jayne."

She had kneeled on the floor beside him noticing how developed his calf muscles were. "Tell me what the feelings were that you tried to drown." She spoke slowly feeling like an ass for taking advantage of the circumstance.

"I was feeling jealous! I am jealous, okay Jayne!" She watched a highly educated, distinguished man, fold his arms across his chest and poke out his bottom lip.

"Are you pouting, Toshi?"

He raised his chin in indignation. "No."

Then thought about it a bit. "Yes." Dropping his chin to his chest as if in defeat. Jayne pulled her office chair over in front of the futon and sat facing him with his, sad, bloodshot eyes looking at her. “It’s not fair.” He leaned back on the futon exposing well-toned and much developed muscled thighs. The towel had fallen down from around his shoulders, exposing a solid chest with perfect pecks and abs which were rock solid. The towel around his waist has also shifted revealing a thin strand of smooth black hair that started under his navel creeping a path underneath the second towel. Her eyes trailed downward, wanting to know more. Jayne grabbed his wet clothing to put in the dryer, removing herself from the temptation to look. Damn that man was sexy.

“Okay, I have your clothes in the dryer. I brought you a pillow and a blanket. Sit in the chair here while I put a sheet on the futon.” He did as he was told, watching her while she worked.

“Jayne, it isn’t fair.”

She continued to work. “What’s not fair Toshi?”

His hand touched the back of her thigh causing Jayne to nearly jump out of her skin. “I touch you like a man. I kiss you like a man and when you are ready…” he hiccupped loudly. “…I will make love to you like a man. My skin tone shouldn’t matter. In the dark, it won’t anyway.”

He laughed again. “When you are screaming my name in the middle of your ecstasy, you ain’t gonna give a flying dragon about the color of my damned skin!” A loud hiccup escaped him. “Oops, filter down! Filter down!” He said it as if giving the warning call of a man overboard.

Jayne saw the obvious pain in his face. With her hands on the towel about his waist, she helped him back onto the futon. The rubber band was removed from his hair, allowing the tresses to fall about his shoulders as she toweled the locks dry. There was no sense in having this conversation with a man who was not in full control of his faculties. Toshi reacted as if he had a *eureka* moment. "I know what it is Jayne. I know what it is."

He leaned forward and poked her in the nose with his finger. "You won't make love to me because you think all Asian men have a small dinky." Jayne's eyes got wide, as she prayed that he would not stand up and try to show her his dinky, or anything else.

"It's not true. Not all Asian men are cursed with a small dinky." He sat there staring into the bathroom door, with his head cocked like the RCA dog, then he squinted his eyes. "Well, not completely untrue." He broke into laughter. "I walked in the bathroom on Phở one time and that man is truly cursed." He laughed harder, holding up his pinky finger. "But don't tell him I told you his secret. He has a minky, inky, pinky dinky! It don't even hang."

He laughed again, leaning back onto the rear of the futon. His face suddenly turned serious. Jayne was trying to figure out what would be said the morning after all of this nonsense. "Jayne, I have a nice dinky."

That was her cue to lock him in this room and leave. He tried to caress her lips with his fingers, but only ended up poking her in the chin with his index finger.

"I know how to use it too!" He scrunched up his face as if he were telling her a family secret recipe. "My dinky is not small." He crinkled his nose while processing another thought. "Well it would appear to be small if you put it next to a big black dude's, but I am perfectly proportioned!" He pointed both index fingers at her as if shooting mock pistols. He then jumped up off the futon, with the towel hitting the floor. "Would you like to see what's behind door number two Jayne?"

She turned her head while yelling at him. "No, Toshi! Put the towel back on!" He ignored her words and walked around her to the hallway to get his wet coat. The black silk briefs he wore left little to the imagination, as he returned with a small grey box in his hands. He nearly missed the futon as he sat back down. Jayne quickly placed the towel over his lap to cover his lower half.

"I am opening my heart to you Jayne." He handed her the Kay's box. She opened it to find a necklace with two open hearts in a Yin and Yang shape.

"I realize you were the Yin to my Yang," he mumbled as he laid back on the futon. "I want it all Jayne and I want it with you." And with that said, Toshi had passed out.

She stared at the diamond encrusted necklace feeling her heart open as well. Her spirit was now open to a drunken Japanese man, who had fallen asleep on her futon, wearing nothing more than a pair of drawers. What would her Grammy say if she saw this?

Chapter 18

Jayne woke to the smell of sizzling bacon, the sound of coffee perking, and a very confused Japanese man standing over her stove.

"Good morning," he said as her poured her a cup of coffee. "I hope you slept well."

"I did, thank you."

Toshi added scrambled eggs along with the bacon slices and a toasted English muffin to a plate and sat it on the table for Jayne. He poured two glasses of orange juice and joined her for breakfast. After blessing the food he opened the conversation feeling foolish for waking up in his underwear in her apartment. "Would you like to discuss last night?"

"No," she said as she sipped at her coffee.

It had not escaped his attention that she was not mad, nor was she throwing him out the door. Around her neck she wore his gift. A bevvy of mixed emotions flooded his chest. One began with the excitement of seeing her wearing his present, but secondly, he felt disheartened that he had not personally placed it about her neck. *Wait! She's wearing it! She didn't get engaged to that other man*?

Jayne's hand went to the necklace, allowing her fingers to run absently over the hearts. "Last night was my first and last date with him. He was attempting to run a game on me and I outplayed his hand." She slid her hand into the pocket of her robe and removed a green box. Toshi opened it to find inside a silver link bracelet which connected with black and yellow koi fishes in a Yin and Yang pattern. Jayne secured it about his wrist.

"I had bought this for you earlier, but I am confused about what that whole drunken display was last night, Toshi," she said as she watched his face take in the surprise of her gift.

Toshi's chest tightened as if it were swelling with something he didn't fully understand. "My feelings for you are running deeper than I had initially realized and it scared me a bit."

Jayne still said nothing as she ate her breakfast. He was feeling vulnerable and she knew it, but she wasn't going to let him off the hook for using booze to get his courage up to come and talk to her about what he was feeling. A real man doesn't do that. "Did you think that loading up on liquid courage was what you needed to come and talk to me?"

Toshi shook his head. "I have made no qualms about my feelings for you. I made those clear the first, second, third, and fourth times I ran into you. However..." he said as he sipped at his tea. "Since spending some real time with you these past months, I have learned to also appreciate the woman. Thereby, altering how I feel about you."

It wasn't working for Jayne. A man who needs to get drunk to deal with his feelings was one she did not need in her life or in her bed. The problem she was facing, was the simple truth that she liked him. She liked him a lot. "Getting drunk and charging over here like a drunken bull in a china shop was the solution for you to deal with your feelings?"

Toshi was shaking his head no. "I was coming over here to fight for you."

Jayne's jaw dropped, then she remembered. "Oh yeah. You were going to kick him in the dick."

His eyebrows shot up. "What?"

Jayne pursed her lips as if to demonstrate how far over this whole thing she was. "Yes, Dr. Yamaguchi. You screamed loud enough for everyone in the building to hear it. *He can't make love to you with a broke dick, Jayne*!"

Neither of them could help, but burst into laughter; the whole thing was so silly. She couldn't find it in herself to be mad at him, plus he had come to fight *for* her. Jayne thought that was simply archaic, Neanderthal-*ish*, and totally romantic.

"I have dreamed about creating this comic book for so long and seeing it come to life is rather scary. I meet you and it feels like everything I ever wanted is approaching fruition all at once. Then I get a phone call telling me you are in a restaurant on Valentine's Day with some dude, saying that you would marry him. I had to deal with my first experience of jealously, as well as the possibility of someone coming along and sweeping you off your feet and taking you from me, before I've even had a real chance to woo and win your heart. Jayne, *I* want to be your man."

Jayne listened to what he was saying. Inside, she had butterflies flitting all over at his words. He wanted to woo and win her? It was dreamy. She liked it more than she could ever admit, but she could not let him off the hook that easy for his behavior. "Jayne, say something. Call me stupid. Say I'm immature, selfish, a prick...something. Just talk to me."

“Toshi, we are business partners. If you and I are never anything else to each other, we are partners on this comic book. The rest we will have to sort out.”

He swallowed hard. “I understand.”

“Also understand that if you ever show up on my doorstep drunk again, I am going to personally call the police on you.”

“I understand,” he said again. “Are you going to hold it over my head?”

“Are you going to try and show me your dinky again?”

He scratched the side of his neck, then his shoulder, and she saw his cheeks turn red. “I did not say that!”

She nodded her head slowly. He lowered his head in shame. Jayne could not help but give him a good swift kick while he was down. “You assured me that it was a very nice dinky and you knew how to use it.”

It was uncertain if he was cursing himself, or cursing at her, but he lapsed into Japanese as he paced the floor in her dining room. He cleared the table, washed the dishes, and put on his coat, still talking out loud in his familial language. Jayne watched in amusement with a smirk on her face. Finally, when he had calmed down, he faced her with his head lowered. “I am sorry for dishonoring you with such talk and behavior. I understand if you never want to see me again. I am truly sorry for showing you such disrespect.”

Jane grabbed him by the front of his still wet jacket. “I have to see you again, Toshi.”

He raised his head to look her in the eyes. “Why is that?”

“You told me that you were working on being a better

man. Based on I what I did see, I agree with you. It looks like a rather nice dinky. I look forward to getting to know it and you a lot better." A small smile returned to his face as she kissed him before sending him on his way.

Chapter 19

March rolled in quietly as Jayne and Toshi completed the designs of the main Vigilante characters for the comic book. Everything was shaping up nicely and both were pleased with the progress. Although they were spending a great deal of time together, neither had pushed the romantic envelope. Jayne was frustrated with the way some of her projects were developing at work and Grammy was pushing her harder to arrange a meeting with Toshi. Frank was also farting more than she could stand.

Toshi swore he was working on his filtering system and often would slip, saying things that he had no business addressing or being entirely too honest at the wrong time. One of these moments happened after the development of the first set of costumes. Jayne was proud of the stitching of the outer legs of the pants for her costume as well as the mesh inlays of the bustier.

"You need to work out some more so those pants will fit right," he told her as he looked up from his desk. Jayne gulped hard to swallow down any personal feelings. He even came to the gym with her one Wednesday afternoon and took out a great deal of aggression on her. Jayne held her tongue.

Her lips only tightened when he spouted off a gem of encouragement by telling her, "You are not working hard enough, Jayne. If you want definition in those abs, you need to sweat and increase your heart rate to burn of some of that fat." *What fat? You tyrannical monster*!

She knew he was frustrated and so was she. They were spending at least three nights a week together sharing nothing more than a few kisses. In the past week, Toshi had withdrawn from even a modicum of affection with her. It was all she had to keep her going and now work was trying to literally suffocate her. Frank's farting was becoming about as unbearable as Toshi's clogged up filters.

It was wrong. Jayne knew it was wrong, but one evening after Toshi had been particularly hard on her, in a week where Frank seemed to intentionally make her miserable, she decided to kill two birds with one stone.

"I will have the new layout ready for you tomorrow, Toshi. Can you swing by my office to pick it up?"

It wasn't difficult to understand the man was sexually frustrated. Jayne thought that maybe a change of pace from working was also in order. "If you have some free time, maybe we can grab some lunch." She was hoping to shift the tension between them.

"Sure," he mumbled. "Thursdays are my short days. I am out of class by 11:50. I could swing by your office at 12:30?" He said it in the form of a question and Jayne was almost giddy in anticipation.

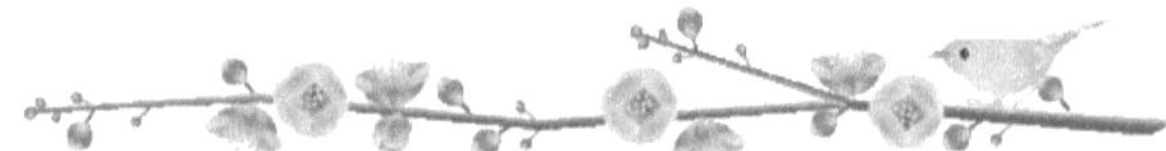

Of the many traits that made Toshi Yamaguchi very likeable in Jayne's book, he was a man of his word and always on time. He arrived at Cawley and Associates at 12:30 on the dot, which happened to coincide with the after effects of Frank's lunch. Rebecca the office manager, directed him to Jayne's desk. She rose to watch his approach down the corridor of cubicles and stood waiting for it.

He hit the invisible wall of Frank's funk and began to twitch as if he had stepped on an electric Taser. His face contorted, while his hands began swinging at an invisible enemy he could smell but not see. He launched into a rant that sounded like the announcer on one of those Japanese games shows. It started with, "Aoohhhh!" Jayne could hear the snickers from the other pod dwellers who also suffered daily from Frank's malevolent malodorousness.

"What is that awful stench?" Toshi asked as he backed up, refusing to come down the row any further.

Jayne waved to him over the top of her cubicle. "I'm back here Dr. Yamaguchi."

"You can stay back there! I am not coming any closer!" He simply stayed put.

Jayne wasn't going to let it go. "I have some new designs on my computer I need you to see."

"You can email them to me," he told her as he started walking toward the front door.

The snickers from the pod people had turned into giggles, but she needed him to get in some one on one with Frank. It took some coaxing, but finally, she got him to travel down the aisle. The giggles had turned to laughter as each cubicle Toshi passed, he poked his head in to sniff, to try to locate the source of the stench. Heads began to pop up over the work stations like Meerkats on the lookout on the desert plains, waiting for Toshi to locate the violator.

As he walked, he sniffed. He took a step, then sniffed. He was only two pods away when Gladys stuffed her scarf in her mouth to dampen her laughter. One cubicle away. The boss had left his office as well to see what was going to happen. Jayne looked down the rows to see whose head was not visible. As soon as Kris Cawley, the VP of Operations came from his office, Tunisia's head was among the onlookers. Leave it to the office busybody to be busy stirring the pot. She had called Kris to come and watch.

Toshi rounded the corner and sniffed the air then came face to face with Frank the Farter. Not only were his filters off, so were the gloves. "Man! What is wrong with you?"

Frank's face had turned red. "Excuse me? Who are you?"

Jayne knew there was no stopping him, but she added some credibility to what he was about to unleash on Frank. "Dr. Yamaguchi, my workstation is over here." This statement he ignored.

He began in Japanese, shaking his finger at Frank, who outweighed Toshi by at least 100 pounds. For some dumb reason, Frank thought it a good idea to stand up to his full height of six feet, hoping to intimidate Toshi who was truly angry. "Sit down you disgusting excuse for a man! How dare you subject your coworkers to such toxic levels of methane! Why? Because you are too lazy to go and have your prostate checked and eat some vegetables?"

Frank mumbled something, which caused Toshi to lapse into Japanese again, reverting to English, back to Japanese then again to English. "You should be ashamed!" It came out like the master sensei in a bad karate movie where he is explaining to the student why fighting for money is wrong.

"You are going to change your diet, eat leafy green vegetables, reduce your carbs, and make a doctor's appointment to have yourself checked!"

Frank was still trying to say something. "Shut up! You listen! You call this man!" He took a personal business card from his wallet and scribbled a number on the back of it, then changed his mind. "No, you go! You go now! See him! Tell him I sent you!"

Frank was almost in tears. "I can't just leave work like that."

Toshi turned to look at all the heads who were staring at him. "Who is this man's boss?"

Kris reluctantly raised his hand. Toshi asked, "do you grant this man permission to leave work early for this appointment that I am setting for him right now?"

Kris nodded. Toshi took out his cell phone and called someone. He spoke to them in his language. He turned back to a red-faced Frank. "He is expecting you. He is on the corner of Davis and Washington road in a white building."

Frank rose slowly and gathered his things, but Toshi stopped him. "You are going to feel much better. Monday will be a better day for everyone in your life."

Frank exited the main doors of the building and cans of air freshener were being sprayed while others clapped and cheered for Toshi. A few people patted him on the back as he looked at Jayne with his arms folded across his chest. He knew she had done this on purpose and he was madder than a wet cat.

Kris Cawley was speeding down the row headed in

their direction. She wasn't sure how it was going to turn out, but everyone in the office was tuned in to the scene. Jayne moved closer to Toshi who had planted his feet, ready for whatever Kris was about to bring.

Kris approached them both. "Jayne. Who is this?" He and everyone in the office wanted to know who this man was that said what they all wanted to, but could not say to Frank. Toshi had given them new hope and for Jayne, he had given her something else. Clarity.

Her fingers laced into his. 'This is Dr. Toshi Yamaguchi," she told her boss. "He is my boyfriend."

Chapter 20

The words uttered in her office to her coworkers, which also defined her relationship with Toshi, was all he needed. He had started to smile again and as she expected, he changed tactics on her once again. The romantic Toshi was unleashed upon an unsuspecting Jayne who, by all accounts, was eating up every minute of his new approach.

He stopped by on Monday morning, on his way to work, with a single stemmed perfect daisy, just to help her start her week out right. He gave her a warm kiss, massaging her neck with his thumbs, then backed away. Jayne was agitated all day. Tuesday, he sent her a selfie of his smile and goatee with the caption, "it happens every time I think of you." He was getting smoother.

After their work out on Wednesday evening, Jayne had a tight muscle in her calf, which he readily volunteered to massage out. He used his vast knowledge of the body's muscular system to explain as he worked. "In order to force the *gastrocnemius* to relax, I must start higher at the *abductor magnus*," he said as his hand slipped between her inner thighs. His fingers probing deep into her flesh, coming way too close to the proximity of her pocketbook. Toshi pushed at her thigh spreading her legs a little further apart, while magical fingers kneaded the back of her thigh.

"Now," he said as one hand worked on her lower calf. His face so inappropriately close to her butt cheek she felt the warmth of his breath. "I will manipulate the bicep *femoris* and stimulate the *semintendinosus*, as I stroke the hamstring." Jayne's eyes closed as she tried to steady her breathing. He was standing upright behind her with waves of heat radiating from his body. She still leaned forward on the workout bench with her butt pointing toward him.

"Jayne, I need you to remove your knee from the bench and bend down and touch your toes." Jayne followed his instructions, feeling his hands upon her hips. She was breaking out into a heavier sweat. His hands were on the back of her thigh, "Focus on the movement of my hands as I caress the *semimembranosus*." Strong, adept hands were burning through the fabric of her workout pants. Just when she was about to tell him that was enough, her calf muscle relaxed. He stepped away. "There. How did that feel?"

It felt like I want some more of that, along with whatever else you got in that bag of tricks. Instead of saying what she was thinking, she played along. "A little more of that and management will be asking us to leave." She laughed as she patted him in the chest, saying good night. She would see him on Saturday night, since she had plans on Friday.

Toshi was not going to be upstaged. He showed up on her office on Friday morning with a perfect red rose and a cup of Bouna Café poured over Brazilian roast coffee. Frank, who was feeling and smelling so much better, was the first to greet him with a hearty thank you and offers of friendship. Toshi had one thing on his mind, only he told Frank he was glad he was feeling better. When he turned his attention to Jayne, he kissed her so completely and thoroughly, that every woman in the office fanned themselves. One even swooned. A few of the men, including Frank, spoke up. "Damn!"

When he departed, Jayne was still out of breath. She was approached by the office busy body, Tunisia. "Girl, if he kisses like that, he must be hell in bed!" Jayne blushed at such forthright talk, especially with a woman who was outside of her inner circle. She gave no answer in words or in tells, excusing herself to get back to work. Her mind was all over the place and so where her hormones. Tunisia's question continued pinging about her brain. Finally, when she could no longer focus, she picked up the phone and called her GYN. She was going to need some birth control...and soon.

On Saturday evening, Jayne was more nervous than a prostitute heading to Sunday service. Instead of being locked away in his apartment, working all close and in a confined space where she didn't know if she would be able to escape his sexy, *come to me baby* approach, Toshi took her on a date. It was nothing fancy. A dinner and a movie kind of date. Jayne was disappointed that they watched the movie and discussed its high points over dinner, with no mention of any special alone time.

Jayne was lost in her thoughts wondering what was wrong, as he walked her to her door. She was totally unprepared for his next move and even more shocked to find out you can kiss someone with your whole body. Which is what he did once he stepped inside her front door.

It seemed so innocent when he stepped forward to take her into his arms, but as his kiss deepened, so did his movements. His arms tightened around her waist as his fingers pressed into the nerves around her spinal column, turning her legs into jelly. When he slanted his mouth over her lips, Toshi moved his thighs against hers as if they were in a slow dance. The thigh movements transitioned into hip movements, swaying from side to side, while he kissed, lifted, and turned her body. Jayne's senses were in overload as his hand slid down her thigh, hefting her leg upward pressing closer to her. *He's right. That is a nice dinky.* The movements were not vulgar or suggestive, but subliminal in the most evil of ways. Toshi broke the kiss, allowing his lips to trail down her neck, to the base of her throat. He gently suckled at her neck, still swaying, pressing, and holding her even closer. The catching of her breath could be heard as his teeth grazed her collar bone. His wayward right hand allowed the thumb to hover just below her right breast. And just as suddenly as he started, he stopped, providing the briefest of kisses and then he said goodnight.

It was not a good night for Jayne. She could not sleep, nor could she forget the feel of his body against hers. This was nothing short of warfare and he was playing dirty. The anger was simmering on the surface, but deep down, she liked how he played. She was ready to get in on the next game. This time, she was dealing.

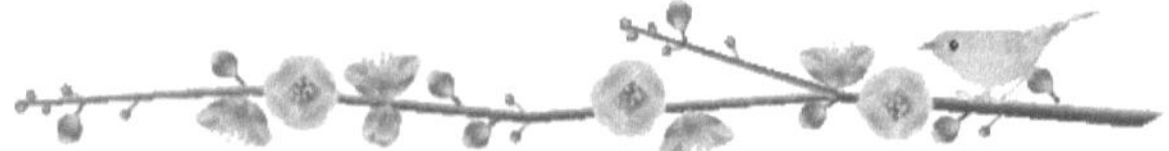

Monday morning brought a new set of worries, troubles, and problems that seemed to be unresolved on her latest ad campaign. If something could have gone wrong, it did. The client hated everything about the concept including the slogan which they provided. Frank was doing his best to lend a hand, but there was no other choice but to scrap the project and start over. Starting over also meant late nights from conception to design. It also meant no Toshi.

Frank was equally unhappy. Since his cleansing through the special appointment Toshi had set, Frank was smelling better and far more pleasant to be around. He started seeing someone in his building. This gave a big spark to his desire to come up with something clever on the cat food campaign which he delivered in a big way. By Thursday morning they were in the black with the client singing their praises. The timing could not be more perfect since Jayne had a doctor's appointment at 9:45. Everything was left in Frank's capable hands as she opted to take the afternoon off as well.

The appointment went fast. By 10:45, Jayne was sporting a new *no kids right now* patch and a saucy attitude. There was enough time for her to swing by her apartment to make a quick change before she placed an order with Yosko for lunch. Food in hand along with a new approach in mind, the drive downtown to the campus cruised along without a hitch. Locating Toshi's office was not as easy.

His business card said he was located on the third floor of the building she was in, as she followed the room numbers, she located his office. "Hi, I am looking for Dr. Yamaguchi," she told the middle age woman behind the desk.

"Dr. Yamaguchi is in class. May I assist you with something?" she asked over the rim of her glasses, eyeing Jayne with some suspicion.

The desk name plate said D. Banks. "Ms. Banks, I

brought him lunch. I thought since today is his short day, I would surprise him." It appeared the one who was more surprised was Ms. Banks who began to sputter over her words. Jayne let the woman off the hook. "I know he is still on the podium, but if I could leave this on his desk and meet him at his classroom, that would be even better."

D. Banks held up both arms each pointing in a different direction. Jayne took it to mean his class was down the hall and his desk was in the rear. "Ms. Banks. After I sit this down, can I get that room number?"

The workspace of Dr. Toshi Yamaguchi looked nothing like any tenured professor's office she had in college. It was organized and it was clean. His desk was not covered by piles of papers or journal articles. It held the faint scent of his cologne, which lingered throughout the office. Jayne checked her watch. There were only a few minutes left in his class and she wanted to surprise him. Ms. Banks handed her the note with the room number on it as she walked by. "We will be back in a few," she told her as her high heels clicked down the hall.

The lecture room wasn't difficult to find. She followed the sound of his voice. Jayne slipped inside the door to take a seat in the rear of the room. The light weight coat was removed to reveal a far too short black skirt and button front form fitting sweater that clung to every bit of the imagination. The stool on the far right was far enough in the rear of the room to not distract the students, but very direct in his line of sight. A cute young female student in the front of the room was pelting him with nonsensical questions. When he looked up, Jayne chose that moment to open and then cross her legs. A slight lean forward onto the table caused his mouth to drop open followed by a very large frozen grin. Every student in the classroom turned to see what had made the professor break his composure.

"That's it for this week. Remember, your outlines of the olfactory nerves are due on Tuesday. Have a great weekend." Although he addressed the students, his eyes never left Jayne or the too short skirt. Mary Elizabeth was still asking questions. Many of which fell upon deaf ears, until finally the young woman asked, "who is that? Your girlfriend?"

Several of the young men were eyeing Jayne whose eyes were transfixed on her man. She licked her lips, silently saying, "hope you're hungry."

One of the men responded, "If he isn't, I sure as hell am. I will take whatever you are serving."

Toshi turned so fast, all of the students jumped. He quickly spotted the wise guy. "You will not disrespect any woman in the classroom Mr. Jones. You will apologize instantly." The embarrassed young man mumbled an apology to Jayne, while Mary Elizabeth watched the professor pack his things and join the guest.

As he approached her, Jayne added in, "I thought I would surprise you with lunch. I brought all of your favorites," she told him in a breathy voice. She turned for him to follow her out the door. Toshi's eyes followed Jayne's perfect ass all the way down the hall to his office. As they both hoped to keep everything above board, the office door was left open. Jayne opened the containers and used the chopsticks to feed him his first piece of sushi.

This she followed with a kiss as she tried to nibble at the sashimi he was holding between his teeth. Her hands became very friendly. Each time she leaned forward, she would stroke his thigh.

A light tap came at the door. Mary Elizabeth had a few more questions for the professor. Jayne wanted the young woman to understand her role in Toshi's life. While his back was turned to answer the young lady, she undid one more button on the sweater as she feigned dropping an ink pen. A bend from the waist in high heels is impressive by any one's standards, but doing so, and picking something up from the floor while showing off cleavage, is a winner. Toshi responded to the student, "go home Mary Elizabeth. Enjoy your weekend. He then closed the door.

"Jayne, Jayne, Jayne." He shook his head as he watched her fiddle with the necklace he had given her. "Whatever am I going to do with you?"

I can think of a few things. She took a seat behind his desk, slowly crossing her legs again. This time revealing the thigh high stockings and the sexy garter. He snapped his fingers. "I got it! Your name should be Gauntlet."

"Is that what you think I just did, throw down the gauntlet?"

"It doesn't matter what you throw at me Jayne. Either way, I am ready to suit up and go all in." His eyes were twinkling as he fed her a piece of the Sierra roll.

"I just bet you are." She toyed with a piece of zucchini, feeding it to him as his eyes followed her back and forth. She swiveled to and fro in the chair. This was definitely a turning point in their relationship. This Saturday night would be very different.

Chapter 21

Disappointment is such an unusual feeling. Especially when it is unclear as to the reason a person senses a letdown. Toshi was uncertain what Jayne had in store for the afternoon. Displeasure was all over his face when she received the call that she was needed back at the office right away. The annoyance Jayne felt became audible as she righted her clothing providing him a hasty kiss in front of the other staff members who seemed genuinely shocked at her presence in his office. Discontentment hung around her neck as she returned to her job to find out that the VP of Operations for Mr. Whisker's Cat Food, did not like the last designs.

Jayne kicked off her shoes and hunkered down. The romantic dinner she had planned had to be cancelled. A saving grace was that her boyfriend was unaware that she had planned to take him out. Dinner instead was a cold sub sandwich on thick bread with a side of wilted lettuce, which was masquerading itself as a salad. Frank wasn't in a very good mood, which caused him some distress. This resulted in the production of some more foul gas. Grammy Pearl always said, *"it doesn't matter your plan. If it is not what God intended, it just ain't gonna happen for you."* Today was one of the only days when Jayne felt her Grammy talked too damned much. They worked until 11 pm and wasn't certain about the new design.

At 7:30 am, she, Frank and Celia, another team member, boarded themselves up in the conference room and worked nonstop on new designs. Kris Cawley sent in sugary snacks, bad pizza, and loads of caffeine at lunch. By 3:30, they had something workable. She and Frank headed back to the drawing board to begin again.

The dissatisfaction in Toshi's voice was evident when he called and was informed that she would be working late. This time, they continued until 11:30, with final touches still needing to be made. As they made their way toward the door, tired and disillusioned, Frank turned too fast and his bag knocked over the ink pots, ruining the boards.

"I am so sorry, Jayne. I am just so damned tired," he said with a sorrowful voice that was followed by a fart.

She couldn't blame the big galoot. It was truly accidental. "We both are exhausted Frank. I will see you back here at 7:30 in the morning."

It took the better part of Saturday to redo the concept boards, shoot the images, and upload the designs to Mr. Whiskers, but it was done. If they hated it, she and Frank would start over on Monday. What she needed right now was a hot shower, some dinner, and her bed. As proud as she was for remaining calm with Frank yesterday, her tension and frustration was compounded as she hit dead stop traffic on Washington Road. Evidently an accident and flashing lights in Augusta, means that everyone should slow down to personally inspect the scene. The fifteen minute drive home was now creeping into 45 minutes and Jayne's knuckles were ashen from gripping the steering wheel. The text message that came from Toshi inquiring if they were still meeting tonight received the response of only, "ggggrrrrrr."

A slow drizzle had started by the time Jayne finally reached home. The gush of rain which followed from the dark clouds drenched her hair, clothing, and spirit as she entered her front door. Even after the hot shower, a glass of wine, and the playing of some Norman Brown, her disposition had not improved. In her comfortable beige leggings covered by an oversized tee, Jayne could not relax. Tension in her shoulders and back prevented her from getting comfortable and she wanted to punch something.

A light tap was heard at the door. Dread crept through her bones as she flatfootedly trudged to the entry to see who was planning to make her evening worse. The look on her face when she open the door made Toshi balk. "I am sorry. I should have called first."

"It's okay. Come on in." There was no enthusiasm in her voice.

As he removed his shoes and sat the bags with their dinner on the counter, he told her, "you look really tense."

Jayne plopped down on the couch. "I am really tired."

Toshi took a seat on the ottoman which was always nestled in the corner but he dragged to the front of the couch, "Jayne, allow me take care of you tonight."

"If you can bring my shoulders down from around my ears, go for it," she said with a hint of sarcasm, but the expression on his face changed her tune. "I hope you can accomplish whatever you have in mind without removing any of my clothing."

A wry smile covered his face, "I will take good care of you Jayne, but first, I need some lotion or body oil."

She was too tired to even sit up, so she pointed toward

the bedroom. "My bathroom...on the sink...choices." She waved her hand as if swatting away a pesky fly.

It was his first entry in her bedroom. It smelled of lavender and lilacs with one wall painted light purple. The quilt which covered the bed appeared to be handmade with bright splashes of vivid colors. The headboard was covered in a bright yellow fabric with small periwinkle flowers with green stems. The furniture was a heavy dark wood that appeared to be antique. A soft rug was by the bed and to his amazement, there were no paintings on the walls. Not even a simple plaque. The bed taunted him like some evil fat kid with the last piece of cake. *This is where she rests that amazing body. What does she sleep in, a gown, shorts, nothing?* The last idea made his body react. *Focus, man....focus...you can't walk back out there with your dinky poking at her.*

In the bathroom, the same color theme continued with a pretty shower curtain, frilly girl towels, and a few items on the counter. He saw the body oil and lotion, opening each and sniffing the containers. Jayne yelled at him. "Stay out from under my sink!" He laughed out loud because when she called to him, his hand was on the door of the cabinet. "Keep out of my medicine cabinet too!"

The jibes were irrelevant to his master plan to move their relationship forward tonight. Armed with only a bottle of body oil, Toshi walked into the living room, perched himself upon the ottoman, and set to work. After tonight, the two of them would form a new connection as a couple.

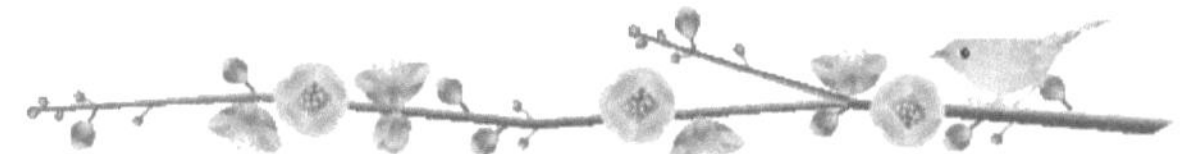

The woman slumped on the couch was not the sexy ingénue that graced his office two days prior. This woman that stared back at him through half open eyes was the cocoon which housed his beautiful Jayne. He was about to set her free.

"Jayne, I am going to do a series of massages on you to release you and free you up a bit. Okay?"

The response was a groan, mixed with a "whatever," and "my panties are staying on Mister."

Her right foot was raised from the floor, with the sole planted in the middle of his chest. Toshi leaned forward to take hold of the bottom of her tee shirt, asking her permission to touch her abdomen before he raised the cotton top exposing her belly while pushing the fabric of the pants down. Warm hands explored her stomach pressing lightly until he found two lumps. Using his index and middle fingers, he applied pressure under both sides of her navel in two quick thumps followed by adding compression in three other spots. Jayne sat up on the couch, eyes wide. "What in the world?"

"Two days of bad food. I moved it forward, so now you should not feel so sluggish." His hand slowly rubbed her calf as he stared into her eyes. "I am also ready for us to move forward as well." He applied pressure to a sore spot on her leg, that she had not been aware was tender. Three swift movements of his hand released the aching spot causing Jayne to say, "Oohh that felt good."

"Lie back and let me work my magic. The rest is going to feel even better," he said as he lifted her foot, massaging the soles with his thumbs. The start of his seductive assault started at her heels, with small circles. Jayne felt her lower region begin to heat up. He locked eyes with her as he pressed deeper, making small, then medium purposeful circles with his thumbs. Fingers enclosed across the top of her feet as his thumbs pressed outward on the foot bones. *Is this supposed to be turning me on? Because it is...it really is.* The warmth she had felt earlier was intensifying, sending signals to her pocketbook to start making change.

Jayne tried to pull her foot back, but he stopped her, massaging the toes. "What are you afraid of Jayne? I move closer, you pull away."

Wide eyes watched him massage her toes. She cooed a bit as he took the big toe into his mouth and suckled it. She swore she could smell everything in the room and feel her ovaries release an egg! His tongue flicked over the neck of the big toe while his hands had moved back to her calf sliding up and down, with the lotion serving as a lubing agent. He nibbled at the meaty portion on the big toe. "Tonight Jayne. We are advancing our relationship. But first, I want you tell me what is holding you back?"

This question was posed as he suddenly grabbed her left leg throwing it over his right shoulder and her right leg over his left. If anyone walked in the room, they would swear they were in the act of coitus. "Toshi, there are some cultural differences between us that can't be ignored. A few of them are serious points of concerns for me." *Like the position I currently find myself in.*

His hands were on her thighs, massaging the tissue of her quadriceps. "Unless we talk about what is on our minds Jayne, we will never grow." He had moved to the ottoman closer which placed her butt in his lap. The heat radiated through the polyester of his running pants. Concentration was escaping through her pores as her body began to respond to his touch. His hands were working her thighs like a bass player in a juke joint. "Damn," was all she could muster at the moment as he lowered her right leg to the floor. What Jayne had been afraid he would see, was now very evident. The seat of her pants were wet. With the light colored fabric, he could see it clearly.

"Now we are getting somewhere," he said as he went to work on her left foot, repeating what he had done to the right. Toes in his mouth and all.

Thoughts pinged about her head as she tried to mentally will her nipples to flatten back out, so she threw something out to throw him off track. "Toshi, our two races are so different. I mean mine came to America on a boat."

It did not stop his tongue from flickering across the neck of her big toe as he responded. "So did mine."

Feeling vulnerable, she told him through gritted teeth, "well my people were in the bottom of the ship rowing it."

He picked her right leg up and placed it upon his shoulder again, using his thumbs to press into the muscle and the base of her glutes. "In some instances, Jayne, mine were as well. If not in the bottom, then in the kitchens cooking and doing the laundry." He pulled her back into his lap, pushing the base of her top upward where it rested under her small breasts, exposing her midriff. His hands were hot as they moved across her taut abdomen, feeling as if he were stealing all of her breath. It did not take him long to spot the birth control patch. An index finger explored the fabric of the patch, letting Jayne know, that he saw it. "Is this new?"

"Yes, I got it on Thursday," she told him as she exhaled loudly.

His hands moved lower, almost touching the top of her girly curls. "So you are thinking what I am thinking as well?"

Jayne couldn't concentrate. "No, I am thinking Toshi, my people built the most of the east coast and the railways to connect to the west." *Why didn't I put on a bra?* She could feel his thumbs now at the base of her breasts, coming close, but not touching. His fingers slid underneath her body, moving one digit at a time along her spinal column as if he were playing a private recital on the ivories. Somewhere between T7 and T18 on her spinal column, he hit a nerve and her legs turned to jelly flopping open at the knees.

"And my people settled the west and built the railroad east to connect with the railways, often dying in camps." His hands moved lower on her spine. Her shoulders were on the couch while the largest part of her was in his lap. "All of that is history Jayne. I am trying to discuss a future." His finger went lower to her lumbar nerves, stroking L1 as he moved down through L5.

"You can't..." she mumbled, trying to say more, but her mouth felt as if she had sucked on a bowl of cotton balls. "...discuss a future, if you can't understand your past, is what I am trying to say. Ooh shit, Toshi. Hit that spot again." Toshi went back to the spot giving it a bit more attention and Jayne moaned out loud. "Yes, that feels so damn good! A bit harder Toshi! Just a bit deeper!" *A few more of those and he is going to see my O face.*

"The past is relevant yes," he told her as he pulled her even further into his lap. "But once you understand its lessons, you can learn and move forward." His fingers were moving down to her sacrum and Jayne was about to lose it. Every nerve in her body was awake and crying for his attention.

"Toshi, this country has not been fair to many races, but mine they enslaved. Now they have imprisoned most of the males, in a sense, enslaving us all over again," she told him as she arched her back giving him more access. The hardened nipples were straining against the cotton of the tee, asking him to connect with them.

Magical fingers crawled up her sides, stopping just outside of her breast before sliding under her shoulder blades. "Jayne, after the bombing of Pearl Harbor, my people were rounded up and placed in concentration camps in Arizona. I know it doesn't compare to slavery, but..." He lifted her shoulders, lowered her legs and she found herself sitting astride him, with her breasts in his face. "...we cannot change our past. I am asking you to move with me; take us forward." His breath could be felt through the cotton of her blouse as his mouth made contact with her breast.

Jayne's hands went into his hair, pulling his head forward as his teeth grazed her nipple through the fabric. "Move with me Jayne," he told her as his fingers slid down to her hips. She shook her head no. In a flash, she found her shoulders back on the couch, Toshi on his knees, and her legs wrapped around him. He lowered his head, planting kisses on her belly. The male scent of him filling her nose. Exciting her more.

His voice was husky with passion as he command her, "Move with me Jayne." She still was not giving as she watched the ebony hair on his head move lower, planting kisses on her abdomen. Her hands flew to the tops of her pants, to hold them in place, "They don't have to come off." Her breath caught as he dropped his head between her thighs, feeling the heat of his mouth on her pocketbook!

"Great day in the morning!" she yelled as she felt the movement of his tongue through the fabric. "Please stop! This is so inappropriate Toshi." The words were said, but her hands were locked in his hair maneuvering his head. She wasn't going to be able to take much more of this.

Evidently, neither could he. He lifted a very petite Jayne off the couch as he stood, turned and took a seat. She stood there looking at him, eyes heavy with passion, craving the finish he had promised. "If you are ready to move our relationship forward Jayne, then come to me and I will help you." The seat of her pants looked as if she hadn't made it to the bathroom on time. His arousal was evident in his gym pants. It had been so long for her. He extended his hand, "I will take care of you Baby, just take the step and show me you want me, Jayne."

She didn't want to seem too eager, but she wanted him in the worst way. Tentatively, she placed her hand in his. Before she could change her mind, Toshi pulled her forward into this arms, kissing her in a way that promised more delights to come. He helped her straddle his lap. The one thing Toshi wanted the most, since he first laid eyes on her, he was finally getting. A handful of the world's most perfect ass.

Fingers sank into her flesh as he showed her how he wanted her to move against him. "Are you ready for me Jayne?"

As their mouths connected, arms enveloped her pulling her close telling her she was home. Fire burned within her belly that ignited something deep within, pulsing through an already excited body craving to win the race. Lips worked feverishly as her hips rocked against the solidness of him trying desperately to reach the unstated goal. She cried out his name as she thrust her hips against his pelvis, unable to achieve the desired feeling she needed. Fingers grappled at his shoulders pulling, pushing, pulling, and pushing until Toshi found himself on his back with Jayne on top of him. Her delicate hands were everywhere as she touched, adjusted and repositioned him to suit her purpose. Satisfied with his awkward position, Jayne let go, throwing her head back as he held on to her hips.

Unprepared for the intensity of her action, Toshi was caught up in her storm and swept along in the current. As she rounded second base for home, Toshi's closed his eyes, going along with the intense ride. The sweet kind woman who seldom raised her voice had turned into a Howler Monkey as she called his name while grunting, moaning, and gyrating against him. Finally spent, she collapsed on top of him as he cradled her in his arms.

The intimate moment was ruined as Timmy made his presence known, growling loudly reminding her she had not eaten. Gentle hands rubbed her back while he whispered in her ear. “If I had my way, I would spend every night for the rest of my life pleasing you, holding you in my arms, and listening to your breath.”

“I think I like letting you have your way with me Toshi,” Jayne told him as she snuggled into his arms and drifted off to sleep. If this was the down payment, she didn’t care what the cost was to get the full ride. She wanted in and she wanted to play.

Chapter 22

It would go down as one of the weirdest days of Toshi's life. His wonderfully intimate evening with his girlfriend ended with him alone on the couch covered in a brightly colored blanket. An initial attempt to empty his bladder became humiliating when he realized he had supermanned himself and his underwear was glued to his pubes. A patch of hair was now missing after he had to cut the material away to get out of his drawers. The cause of his pain had evidently left for church and didn't want to wake him.

In a hurry to make it to church himself, after his shower, he forgot to put on a pair of underpants and was free balling it for the remainder of the afternoon. In church, Kunio kept passing notes, which he refused to read, forcing his father to give the naughty boy finger shake to him. Even at 30 years old, he found himself mouthing, "She started it!"

The afternoon got weirder as his sister pelted him with questions about Jayne. Where she worked, what she liked to eat, and her favorite color. "Lavender, why?" Kunio would not divulge what she was up to and his neck hurt from sleeping on Jayne's hard couch. A slow smile crept across his face during the familial late lunch as he remembered last night, which made his mother burst into tears. She had been doing that a lot lately and he wondered if something was wrong.

Not to be dismissive, he kissed his mother good bye, threw a pine cone at his sister's head and headed home, only to find Raheem waiting on his door step red-eyed, hung over, and looking like a homeless St. Bernard. Toshi escorted his friend inside, encouraging him to open up. The words were immediately regretted, as Raheem began to discuss intimate details of his relationship with someone name Raoul. Of the 43 muscles located in the face, none of them moved as the details became more graphic, ending with his friend of many years, in tears once more. It appeared that Raheem confessed his love after some intense sex, in which Raoul did not respond. The lack of clarity in the conversation made 8 of the muscles in Toshi's face twitch, because his friend could have skipped the details on their sex life to get to the problem. Raheem was embarrassed.

"That is nothing my friend," Toshi told him as he poured him a fresh cup of tea. "I am so far gone with Jayne, I came in my pants last night and supermanned myself to my underwear and had to cut a strip of my pubic hair out this morning to remove my spunked up drawers."

The low rumble of laughter seeped up through Raheem's chest coming out in a gut busting laugh. Raheem laughed even harder when Toshi stood, partially unzipped his pants and showed him the reverse landing strip he had given himself. "Yeah, you are probably thinking the same thing. That was a massive load. It has been a while since I had some loving." Which made Raheem fall over on the couch in guffaws. This prompted Toshi to tell his friend, "let your words marinate with Raoul. He will respond when he's ready. Now shut up. At least you are getting some."

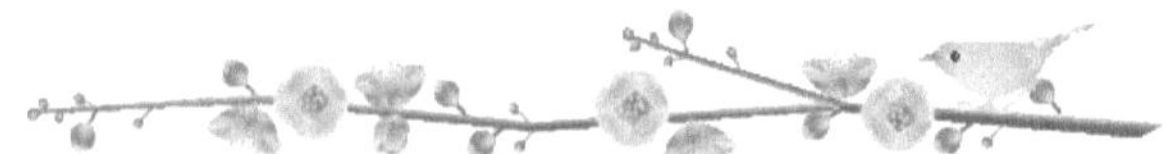

Grandma Pearl swore she could smell sin and she could smell that Jayne had gotten some as well. Jayne allowed the family matriarch to ramble. It was far easier than telling her she hadn't actually copulated with Toshi. This was followed by a litany of questions about why she had not been to any cons lately.

"I am planning to go Los Angeles in July to debut our new comic book," she told her Grammy as she helped set the table.

Grandpa Joe, who swore he was deaf in one ear from a bombing in Viet Nam, turned in his seat. "Who is 'our', Chile? That implies some plurality."

"Toshi and I are debuting our comic book in Los Angeles," she said, which caused Grandma Pearl to jump up and head toward the prayer closet. "We will have separate rooms Grammy. What is the big deal?"

"The big deal, Miss Hot in the Pants, is that you are traveling across the country with this man, who may turn out to be a serial-killer-rapist, who wants to tie you up and eat sushi off your boobies!"

Grandpa Joe and Jayne had the same expression of the *what the frack Pearlie?*, plastered on their face. "Grammy seriously. He lives in the same complex I live in. He works at the university and he is a nice guy."

"He ain't that nice. You haven't brought him by here to meet us," Grandpa Joe mumbled.

"Yes, Missy. Before you go and get on any plane with him, we need to meet this man," Grandma Pearl said as she called them to the table for her mushy meatloaf.

"No problem. I will make that happen," she assured them both as she sat at the table, eyeballing the greasy cabbage. How was she going to tell Toshi her folks were ready to meet him. Hell, how was she going to explain…her folks?

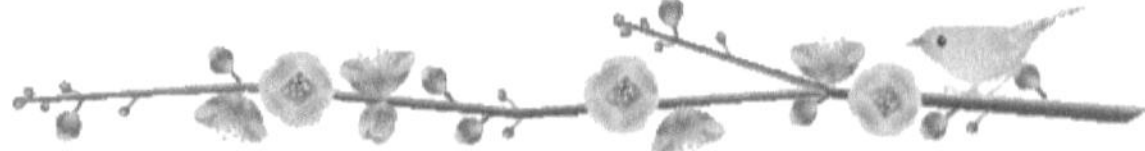

On Tuesday morning, Tunisia routed a call to her desk. "This is Jayne Wright. How may I help you?"

There was a moment of silence on the phone, but she could hear someone breathing. She repeated herself. "Jayne Wright. May I help you?"

"So sorry Jayne. Someone was talking to me. This is Kunio Yamaguchi." It was an honest response when Jayne told her it was a pleasant surprise. Her mind shifted to a worst case scenario. "Is Toshi okay? Has he been hurt?"

It had not entered Kunio's mind that a call out of the blue from her could cause a panic. She wanted to calm her down. "As far as I know, that lunkhead is fine. I would like to run over him with my car sometimes, but no, all is well." This was followed by a pregnant pause. Jayne was busy with no time to play a guessing game with her. "What can I do for you Kunio?"

"I am uncertain if you are aware, but next Friday is Toshi's 31st birthday. We usually have a family dinner at the house. I was wondering if you were free to join us."

Jayne wasn't aware that it was his birthday, but to keep from feeling stupid… "Sure what time? We are supposed to meet up with our friends later that night for some dancing. You are more that welcome to join us as when we go out."

"I would love to. I will bring my fiancé as well," Kunio told her, then provided the address to the Yamaguchi home and dinner time for next Friday. Jayne only had about ten days to get things in order. First on the list was planning some dancing with their friends. A present was also needed for her boyfriend. What could she give him? As she looked about her cluttered work desk, she spotted the corner of the layout boards for the comic book. A gigantic smile covered her face. Perfect. Now on to the friends.

She remembered that Phở worked for King's Beauty Supply, prompting a call to the main store. On her first attempt, someone hung up on her. The second attempt she pretended to be a new beauty shop opening and was connected immediately. Phở was excited about her idea and would take care of calling Felix and Raheem.

"Ah, Phở." Jayne asked, "where does Toshi like to go to dance?"

"The Country Club is his preference, but we don't stay long because of his students who also go there." Phở told her as a warning.

After chatting for a few more minutes with Phở about her idea, she called her girlfriends and provided them with a time and location. All was ready, with one exception. She had no idea how a Japanese family conducted dinner and she was about to meet his parents!

Holy crap! She was about to meet his parents! A slow thought began to burn in the back of her mind. An idea so ingenious, that it would set a new record for the best birthday present in the whole, wide world. A second thought began to burn in her as well. She was going to make his birthday perfect.

Chapter 23

Nearly four days had passed since her intimate relaxation session with Toshi. In all honesty, she was afraid to be alone with him. If that man could turn her on like that fully dressed, she shuddered at what he could do without her clothing. As the week progressed, the Wednesday workout went well. He complimented her body on the new definition in her arms and thighs.

Thursday, he brought lunch to her office and spent good deal of time chatting with Frank about nutrition, work out plans, and water consumption. Frank's admiration for Toshi extended to the work completed on the comic book. Jayne showed him a few of the concepts and layouts telling him she needed to go to press. Frank made a phone call to a few friends, which changed everything. Jayne was in his debt and physically hugged and kissed the man for his contribution. Things were rolling far better than she had hoped.

On Friday, Jayne surprised Toshi by taking him on a date to M.A.D. studios where they listened to live jazz with Karen Gordon and the Method. He seemed a bit distracted all evening, until finally she had to ask what was troubling him.

"My birthday is next Friday," he said in a low voice.

"Okay," she told him quietly.

He exhaled, almost dreading what he was going to say next. "My parents usually plan a family dinner." Jayne said nothing as she stared at him, waiting to see where he was going with this statement. "I would love if you could attend."

"I'd love to," she told him. "Can you please pass the pepper?" The look on his face read as if he expected her to say no.

"You are okay with coming to my parents for dinner?"

"Yes! It's no problem, I am looking forward to meeting them," she answered as she sampled some of the shrimp on his plate. It concerned her that Kunio hadn't mentioned to him that she had already been invited.

"Just like that? You are okay to meet my parents?"

"Sure. Are you okay and ready to meet mine? Which you have to do before we leave for L.A.," she added with a smile.

"I'm okay with that." He was smiling back at her.

"One thing though," she said as she watched his expression grow somber. "I have no real knowledge of Japanese customs and I don't want to do anything to offend your parents."

Toshi's expression was warm, loving, and genuine when he reached across the table to hold her hand. "Just be yourself, Jayne."

"I can do that." She smiled back at him. Jayne didn't know any other way to be, which worked out flawlessly.

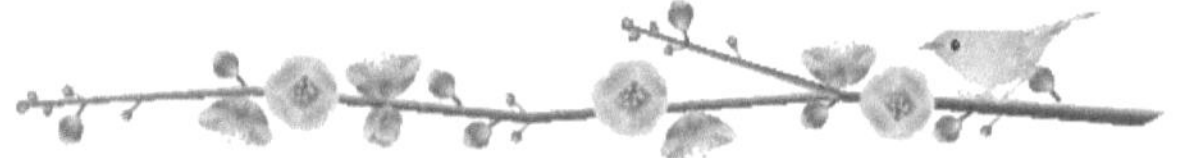

The week sped by and soon Friday was upon her, leaving Jayne as nervous as a Hobbit at the church foot washing. She opted for a simple black skirt, a cream colored twin sweater set, and mid heeled pumps. Toshi had no idea that they were going dancing later. Tear drop pearl earrings were added to her ears and the necklace he had given to her for Valentine's Day. Her hair was put in an up do, with the wispy locks appearing almost managed. A smidgen of gloss was added to her lips. As she rode beside him in the car, her legs trembled so much, she had to put his present on the back seat out of fear she would shake the wrapping loose. By the time they pulled into the drive, she was so nervous, her bladder felt as if it was going to burst.

The family home was located in Evans in the Jones Creek subdivision. It was a European style home that Toshi said had only four bedrooms. The outside of it looked like there should be more. "I usually park around back, but since this is your first visit, we will go through the front door." Although she nodded, Toshi could see she was extremely nervous, which was totally unlike the bold confident woman he had spent the better part of eight months trying to woo and win.

"Jayne, relax. They are just parents." She nodded, but looked as if she was going to throw up. "Tell me what you are so concerned about."

Her lips were pressed closed as she mumbled that she had to pee. Toshi burst into laughter as he pulled her into his arms after planting a kiss on her forehead. "Come on inside." He pulled her by the hand into the living room. Jayne was surprised. It was very modern, with only hints of Japanese styling. Kunio was the first to spot them and gave Jayne a big hug. Toshi, she socked in the arm. "Mom, Dad. This is Jayne. Jayne this is my father, Hirishito Yamaguchi and my mother Eri."

Jayne kowtowed to them both. "Hirishito, like the

restaurants," she said as she smiled at his father.

"You have dined in my restaurants, Jayne?" Hirishito asked her with his bushy eyebrows raised.

"I have eaten there often Sir, but I had no idea that the chain belonged to you," she said as her attention turned to his mother. "Mrs. Yamaguchi, you have a beautiful home. Thank you for inviting me." Kunio pulled her by the arm to meet her fiancé, Dr. Akira Fujimoro. It was difficult for Jayne not to stare at the man. He had the largest head she had ever seen on a human. Toshi pulled her to the side and whispered in her ear, "I warned her not to have his children, or she would be ruined for the rest of her life. I told her I wouldn't claim the big headed little monsters as my kin."

It was said with such a straight face that Jayne wasn't sure if he was kidding, until he cracked a small smile. She playfully hit him in the arm. His parents called them into dinner. The dining room was magnificent, but as Jayne peeked around the corner, the kitchen made her catch her breath. Her entire apartment could fit in the open kitchen. It had the latest Sub Zero appliances and a stove that Jayne longed to cook something on. "Mrs. Yamaguchi, this kitchen is amazing!"

Eri smiled with pride as she asked Jayne to lend her a hand with the food. She kept her eye on Kunio so she could follow her lead, but dinner was simple. The food was Teriyaki Chicken with vegetables and rice. Just as she was about to relax, she felt Hirishito's eyes upon her. His mother was saying something in Japanese to his sister and based on Toshi's facial expression, he didn't like it. Jayne was raised by a woman, who didn't believe in biting her tongue, so it seemed only appropriate to be herself as she had been instructed. "Kunio. Does your mom have a question for me?"

Toshi shook his head and squeezed her leg, but Jayne wanted to know. Kunio sat like the cat holding the canary and spilled the beans. "Our mother is convinced that you used some black girl sex tricks to hook Toshi."

Jayne blinked several times and swallowed hard as the rosy tinge of embarrassment crept up her neck filling her face with redness. She would not balk. "Mrs. Yamaguchi, I have no carnal knowledge of your son," she told her as she dropped her eyes to her plate. Every eye at the table turned to Toshi, who shrugged and continued eating his dinner. Hirishito opened the conversation with the next question. "What made you decide to date our son?"

Jayne slowly raised her head. "He was willing to fight for me." She slipped her hand into Toshi's as she recounted his coming over, soaking wet, declaring his intentions. "He was fueled with a bottle of Sake and on a mission. If there was a man in my apartment, he was going to ensure that poor guy would never reproduce." Eri's hands flew to her face while Hirishito began to sit up tall. Jayne continued. "There was no other man. He had it all wrong, but he was willing to fight for me and to call me his own." She rubbed his hand. "Before he passed out on my futon, he gave me this on Valentine's night." She showed them the necklace. "Letting me know his heart was open to me."

Toshi frowned at her. "I can't believe you told them that story." Since there was no sex involved, Eri, now curious wanted to know more. "Toshi. What made you want to date Jayne?"

"She gets me," he said as he finished his dinner. "She showed up one day, out of the blue and brought me all my favorites for lunch." Eri fought back her tears and waited for him to say more, but that was all he had to say.

Jayne filled in the gap. "I don't see how anyone else's Teriyaki Chicken can compare to what your mother has cooked tonight. This is so delicious Ms. Yamaguchi." Eri, was also now sitting up tall, feeling the pride of having been praised for her cooking, as well as now knowing her son's favorite entrée.

Jayne looked at her watch and nodded to Kunio that things needed to speed up a bit so they could meet the others. "I will help you clear the table so we can give Toshi his presents." Before the gifts were presented, Jayne poured Toshi a cup of tea and he thanked her with a brief kiss on her cheek. It was such a small gesture to the two of them, but to his parent's watchful eye, the two shared a great deal of time together.

As the gifts were presented, Toshi's lack of facial expressions only exacerbated the banality of the gift exchange, which Jayne found completely unacceptable on his part. His mother's gift of a new shirt was met with a disenchanted, glazed over stare, but Jayne touched the shirt. "Oh, I love this material. This will look really good with your navy slacks or even those black jeans." Toshi eyed the shirt again. "You're right. It would." The bracelet that was given to him by Kunio, she placed on his wrist, removing the one she had given him for Valentine's Day and putting it in her purse. His father gave him a set of cooking knives. Jayne teased that Mr. Yamaguchi would have to teach her how to make his perfect knife cuts.

"I'll teach you Jayne." Toshi added, almost seeming defensive that she asked his father instead of him.

"I know, but he *is* the Master Chef and every woman wants at least one cooking lesson from a Master Chef, just to have the bragging rights." Her hand stroked his arm as she gave her response. Both father and son saw the validity of her point, with Hirishito nodding.

Jayne was the last one to present her gift. All eyes were upon her as she handed the box to Toshi, who opened it to find an iPad. The look of confusion on his face was noticeable, as he eyed Jayne with some concern. He had a laptop which converted to a tablet, and a MacBook. Why would he need an eReader?

"No, sillyhead. The iPad is mine. I put it in there to show you this." Her finger swiped the screen and it opened to an Amazon page. Jayne made a few taps to the screen and an e-version of *The Vigilantes* came up. Toshi's eyes were wide. "It went live two weeks ago," she told him as she tapped on the screen again, logging into another page. "Since last week, we have sold 270 copies!" Toshi was still quiet as he stared at the screen, but Jayne was not done.

She pulled up the webpage, the Facebook page, and the Twitter accounts. "You have followers on Twitter, fans on Facebook, and the webpage is just waiting for some more input from you."

"Jayne, this is amazing, how…?"

"It would appear that Frank is your biggest fan. He

made a few phone calls and helped me get these done for you." She moved the iPad and pulled out the first three editions of *The Vigilantes* comic books. The box was removed from his hands as she gave him the three copies of the books. "Of course, we have some editing to do before final printing, but it is live and real, Toshi. We even have advertisers!"

The room was quiet as everyone watched his face as he opened the page of the first issue. His mother gasped when she saw her son use his thumbs to flick away the tears which had started to roll from the corner of his eyes. The flow of salty liquid emotions increased as he went from the first issue to the next, and then the next. Jayne dropped to her knees in front of him, pulling the handkerchief from her sweater sleeve to wipe his face. "Happy birthday baby," she told him, as emotion filled eyes gazed at her.

"How did you get all of this done so fast?"

"I just threw down the gauntlet and cracked the whip to make this happen for you."

He dropped the comics and reached down to pull her up into his arms. He held her close, rocking slowly, whispering in her ear. As suddenly as he grabbed her, he pushed her to the side. His arm flung about her shoulders, speaking to his family in Japanese. Everyone smiled, so Jayne did as well. "I don't know what he said but it must be something good!" She looked at her watch. "Doc, Kunio, Toshi. We have to run." She issued an apology to his parents for having to cut the evening short, promising to come again. Even implying that they would have them over as well.

"Where are we going Jayne?"

"Part two of the surprise Birthday boy. Let's get going!" As they said their farewells, Jayne puled Kunio to the side. "What did he say?"

She hugged Jayne. "He presented you to us as the woman he has chosen to share his life."

"Oh, that's nice," Jayne told her as she tried to quell the butterflies dancing in her stomach. *The woman he has chosen to share his life.* Her more immediate concern was if she was ready to share to his bed. Tonight, she would find out.

Chapter 24

They arrived at the Country Club a few minutes after ten to find both sets of their friends in the corner, at a very large table decorated with balloons. Felix had brought his wife and to the surprise of many, Raheem had brought Raoul. Everyone seemed to have a partner or date, with the exception of Phở and Tamika, who paired up for a few dances. Jayne introduced Kunio to her friends as well as Akira, whom Tamika already knew. No one broached the subject, but she openly admitted, "he's my dermatologist." A resounding, "Ooohhh," went through the group, in almost a form of relief. Tamika whispered under her breath, telling the group to bite her.

Phở leaned in to Jayne whispering, "you want to see something amazing?" He held up a finger and went to the DJ booth, then came back, obviously pleased with himself. "Just wait for it." The conversation was all but forgotten until *The Wobble* came on and Toshi jumped up. "That's my jam right there!" He took off for the dance floor. Jayne, her friends and even Kunio's eyes were wide as they watched him improvise the line dance moves, almost gliding across the wooden floor, stepping, winding, dipping and wobbling like a pro. Watching him move brought on a flood of memories of her couch, with Toshi asking her to move with him. The more she watched him, the more she wanted to truly move with him.

Some of his students were in the club and came over to join him. Jayne immediately recognized the young woman who had followed him to his office the day she was there. *Unacceptable.* He hadn't even noticed them until the music stopped and a slow country song came on, prompting Jayne to head out onto the floor, slipping her arms around his waist.

"Thank you for a wonderful birthday Jayne. I am almost speechless and to be here with our friends to celebrate, it can't get any better." He lowered his head to kiss her, still shifting from side to side with the music.

"After seeing you move like that on the dance floor, I think the evening can get much better. You ready to get out of here?"

Toshi looked at her trying to ascertain if what she said was an invitation to something more. The student was still trying to get his attention, but Jayne had had enough. "Sweetheart, he is your professor. His job is to train and educate you to get a job in your chosen field." Mary Catherine looked hurt, but Jayne wanted to ensure the young lady understood. "Every woman deserves a man that sees her for who she actually is and that man should want to spend every day of his life making you happy. That man is out there waiting for you to notice him."

Mary Catherine's mouth dropped open, but before she could respond to Jayne's words, Toshi returned and picked Jayne up off her feet and carried her to the table. They said their goodbyes and headed for home. The silence in the car was too thick for either of them to breath. The club was only minutes from their complex. Toshi walked her to the door.

"Aren't you coming inside?"

"I don't think that is a good idea. Not in my current state of mind," he said in a lowered tone.

"What state of mind are you in?" She moved closer to him, touching the buttons of his shirt.

Filters on, Toshi. Filters on. "Jayne, I just don't think it is a good idea." *If I come in there, those panties are coming off.*

Jayne kicked off her shoes, removed her sweater, and wiggled her finger at him, beckoning him forward. He was still shaking his head. "I'm not prepared, Jayne."

Her hands slipped under her skirt and removed her underwear, stepping out of them one leg at a time, them throwing them at his face, "I also took that basket of goodies out of the garbage can and put it under my bathroom sink."

She walked away slowly, making her way to the bedroom. She heard the living room door click and he took off his shoes. The soft footfalls could be heard following her. Jayne turned on the bedside lamp and she stared at him standing in her doorway.

"Jayne, this is your last chance to send me home," he told her in a low voice. Her response was to remove her sweater and drop it on the floor next to the discarded matching cardigan. A quick trip to the bathroom, then she dumped the contents of Brionna's love kit on her bed, taunting him. Toshi accepted the challenge.

In two steps he had crossed the room and had Jayne in his arms, lifting her and dumping her on the bed. Her breath caught from the impact with the mattress, but he took her breath away when she felt his mouth on her pocketbook. His tongue moved expertly raising her arousal level from lukewarm to burning hot. His fingers were like magic as he explored, delving into her inner most sanctum, releasing her inhibitions. Toshi caught her inner labia between his index and middle finger, exposing the queen in the tower, who poked her head out only to be suckled by a very hungry man. "Dear Heavens!" Jayne cried out as she pressed her lady parts to his mouth, begging for more. His mouth increased the pressure, while his fingers probed deeper and his tongue flicked back and forth across the nub of flesh. She couldn't hold it any more. She cried out his name as she bucked against his mouth.

Slowly, he disengaged himself from her legs to stand and remove his shirt. Jayne watched him from the bed. Eyelids heavy with passion, but he stopped as he reached for his belt buckle. She bounded from the bed to lend him a hand, pushing the slacks down over his waist, tugging at his underwear. He was ready for her. As she reached for him, hands which were trembling, caught her wrist.

"What's wrong, Toshi? You want my mouth? I don't really know how to do it, but you could teach me how...you know.... to please you....." He chuckled as he pulled her in close. The hardness of him pressing against her belly.

"It's not that Jayne, I just ...." his voice trailed off.

"I sense some hesitation Toshi. You don't want to be with me in this way?" Her voice trembled with emotion as she tried to pull away from him.

His mouth captured hers in an all-consuming kiss. "I have wanted to be with you from the first moment I saw you Jayne. I want you so bad that it is scaring me a little.

I don't want to….."

"What? Go all Super Saiyan on me?"

He could only hold her close as he tried to process the emotions and choose the properly filtered words, but Jayne wanted him to make love to her. "Oh for goodness sake, Toshi! Forget the filters and just say what is on your mind."

Fine! If that is what she wanted, he would tell her exactly what he was thinking! "Jayne, I want this to a beautiful experience between us, but honestly…" he paused, catching his breath. Her eyes wide waiting to hear his words. "I just don't want to get too rough or hurt you."

Jayne responded by removing her skirt and letting it fall to the floor. Next she removed her bra and stood in front of him in all of her glory. If she had not been watching, she would not have believed it as his dinky seemed to grow at least two more inches. "This is truly a nice dinky," she told him as she sat down on the bed, pulling him forward. She hand stroked him up and down, giving extra attention to the sensitive head.

Those were a few of her last understandable words. He used her bed pillows as support under her stomach as she lay face down, uncertain of what was coming next. He positioned himself at the back of her thighs. His legs outside of hers. He made his initial entry, only to withdraw and come in again at another angle. He did this several times until he was able to work himself completely inside of her. Jayne felt so full of him. He pressed, withdrew, pressed, withdrew as if he were looking for something. It did not take her long to comprehend he was looking for her G spot and a few strokes later, he had located it. This, Jayne was certain of, because the only thing that came out of her mouth was gibberish G-words starting with, "good gracious!"

Followed by, "gobstoppers," then "grapesickle." This was followed by, "googobgabgrettt," which was closed out by and inaudible, "grrrggrggggeeggggggeee!" *I plan to give you hours of pleasure*, flashed through her mind as she reached her second climax. He wasn't done. Toshi turned her to her back. "Jayne." he whispered her name as he plunged into her again, dropping his head to her neck, kissing, nibbling suckling. "You feel so amazing. I can't even...." His voice became hoarse as he rolled his hips under, and thrust upward. Jayne's nails dug into his back. Each stroke, he seemed to go deeper inside her sugar walls. He pushed her into a reclining lotus position and Jayne thought she couldn't take any more.

"Toshi...stop please...please stop." She cried out as she bit into his shoulder.

"Am I hurting you Jayne? Are you okay, Baby?" She was fervently shaking her head no. "Tell me. Am I too rough? Is it uncomfortable?"

"I don't know, Toshi. I...." Her voice was smothered by his mouth as he kissed her again, withdrawing himself a bit. She pulled her mouth away from his, breathy, excited, feverish, "Is it supposed to feel this good?"

"If I am doing right, then yes it is." He kissed her again, whispering words of praise. Entering her slowly, methodically, inch by inch filling her up.

She dug her nails into his lower back. "You are soooo, doing it right! Good heavens, you are doing it right!" He laughed a bit as he pushed again, plunging deeper, forcing her to throw her head back, arching her back in the air. Toshi did not miss the obvious opportunity to capture a tight bud between his teeth. Jayne was almost beyond reason.

Through labored breathing, Jayne asked, "Toshi, is it okay if I move with you?" She demonstrated this by rolling her left hip upward. He dropped his head to her neck, withdrew, and plunged in deeper still, only to have her right hip come up to meet him. He lapsed into Japanese, looking her in the eyes and he thrust harder, talking to her, thrusting, and staring deep into her eyes.

"That sounded dirty," she told him as she pulled the rubber band from his ponytail, which allowed his hair fall freely about his neck and shoulders.

He still stared into her eyes as he moved inside of her, "it was was...but it just feels so..." he repeated what he had said earlier in Japanese, still thrusting, holding her hips, while trying to get deeper, wanting to be one with her.

With a handful of his hair in her hands, she pulled his head to her breasts. Shoving a mound into his mouth, while instructing him on what and how she needed him to take care of it. The more he moved the hotter her body was becoming.

"You feel so good inside of me too, Toshi….so good!" Jayne began to pick up the pace of her movements, forcing Toshi to do the same. "So damn good!"

"Slow down a bit Jayne. I can make it last longer." She would not hear it. What she whispered in his ear next, pulled the red flame that had been burning inside him from the recesses of his life givers. The fire which he often spoke of, had been tapped, sprayed with an accelerant and making a trail toward to his sweet Jayne. Stroke after stroke, he tried to go deeper as she clung to him, meeting each of his thrust with one of her own. He felt her body clamp down around him, pulling him in, milking him, forcing the flame up, upward, seeking, looking, pulsating, red, hot fire, throbbing, pushing, thrusting, squeezing, seeking. "Jayne!" he growled as he sensed the red flame turn blue.

"More Toshi! Give me more!" she cried as she shoved her hips upwards against his, biting at his arm, kissing on his skin while tugging at his hair. "Harder, Toshi, harder!"

Her legs locked around his waist as she met him with an intensity that scared and elated her at the same time. She couldn't believe she was having a third orgasm and she bit at his chest to keep from screaming. Toshi's cry was primal as he reached his climax, thrusting, pushing, and trying desperately to get it all out. Jayne began to howl as she shuddered against him, locking her legs about his waist.

He collapsed on top of her, completely spent. *This is the woman I have chosen to share my life with, dear Lord I only hope I survive nights like this.* His arms cradled her close not wanting to let go. Still inside. Not wanting to come out. Slick with sweat and saturated in ...happy.

He had been waiting for this moment. Playing with the idea of what it would be like and willing to pay whatever cost she commanded. It was well worth the wait. Jayne had exceeded his expectations and the realization that something magical had occurred, surrounded him. “Simply amazing,” he told her as he pushed sweat soaked curls away from her face.

Chapter 25

The weight of him could be felt as he left the bed, leaving a coolness on her back where his body had lain. Her eyes would not open out of hesitation that the fairylike spell would be broken, Toshi would turn into a frog and she would be ugly with a huge wart on her nose. Instead, she lay in the shadowed bedroom, listening to his movements. A wry smile crossed her face as she heard him lower the toilet seat down. Still Prince Charming. The water could be heard trickling down into the tub along with his fingers, splashing, testing the liquid's temperature. *Is he about to shower and leave?*

Soft footfalls on the carpet were heard as he made his way to the kitchen, filling what sounded like two glasses with ice and water. Jayne still had not moved, even when he came back into the bedroom and took the glasses into the bathroom. Curiosity was eating her alive, but she would not open her eyes. Seconds later, he returned to the bed. The mattress giving under the weight of his knee as his arms reached for her, scooping her up, cradling her head to his chest like a babe. She could still hear the water running. He raised his right leg to step up, find his balance and then bring up his left leg, only to lower them both into the warm water. Jayne's eyes flew open.

Toshi had lit the candles around her tub. They were now in the bathtub together! *How absolutely romantic.* "That was smooth," she told him as he turned her in the tub so her back would lean on his chest. His hair was still unbound and she had not realized how much hair he actually had until she looked back at him again. The bath sponge, that was seldom used, he placed under the water and they both watched as it soaked up the liquid. Toshi squeezed the loofa, forcing the water out, and watched it run down her breasts. The water continued to rise around them until it reached a comfortable soaking level. The bubbles now coming up and resting underneath her breasts before he turned it off.

"So..." speaking softly to him. "...that is what I have been missing for the past 8 months?"

His arms rested on the back of the tub. "There is a big difference in having sex with a guy you sort of like and being intimate with the man you love."

Jayne turned suddenly in tub, splashing water onto the floor. "Really? The man I love? And how did your analysis of the data bring you to that conclusion Doc?"

Toshi grabbed her leg, pushing her backwards, using her own body's buoyancy to manipulate her in the large tub. "You would never give me your body Jayne, unless I had earned your heart."

She watched him with some amusement as he raised her foot and took her big toe into his mouth. "So based on that, you believe that makes me love you?"

He pulled her closer to him. Their naked bodies creating ripples in the water. "Between that, and my ability to make you howl like a monkey," he dragged out the word howl. The low rumble of laughter reverberated in his chest.

Jayne gave a slight push with her foot, mushing her toes into his lips. "I hate to say this, because I know it will give you the big head, but man....." She paused as she watched him massage the ball of her foot. "That *was* really good." Her face became serious as she withdrew her foot from his hands, leaning forward with her fingers upon his thighs. Through lowered lashes she asked the question, "did I please you Toshi?"

The answer was gradual in coming as Toshi began to kiss her slowly, taking his time to form the right words to say out loud what he was thinking. "Every day, every hour, every minute I spend in your light, pleases me. You please me Jayne. More than that, you make me happy."

The other questions that pinged about in her brain would have to be answered at another time. The only thing that mattered now, were the two of them.

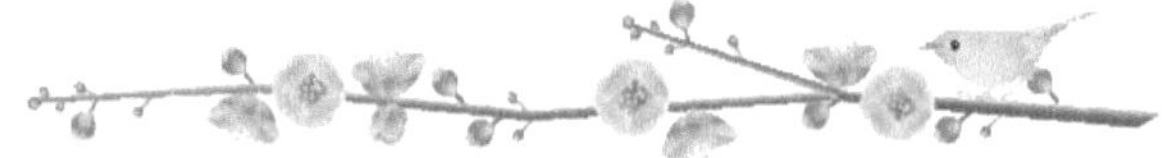

It was the oddest damned thing. Toshi had a sensation that something was missing. He was due to meet the guys at one o' clock, but he could not focus. A mind filled with conflicting ideas buzzed about, hindering his ability to capture a single thought. Waking up with Jayne in his arms and her head nestled against his chest, sent ripples of emotions through him that he couldn't fully process. The feelings were too new and created a feeling of vulnerability.

The comic books she had given him last night, were all but forgotten, until he remembered he left them at his parent's home. A quick swing through to pick up those and Jayne's tablet before he met the guys, had to happen. More surprising than his new state of mind, was the surrealism of his father being home on a Saturday morning, sitting at the table. Reading his comics.

"Toshi. Is this what you have always wanted to do?" Hirishito asked with some confusion.

"Yes, but I knew I could not dishonor you to call it a career. But yes, Father, it is something I have dreamed of creating." He spoke softly as he took a seat at the table.

"And this woman...?"

"Jayne, Father. Her name is Jayne," he said with his head lowered.

Hirishito eyed his son's face. "This Jayne...helped you create this?"

His eyes sparkled as he gently removed the first edition from his father's hands, explaining the art work, storyline, and showing off his drawings. "The color work and storyline was done by Jayne, but here..." He pointed to the main character Katsuo, "...are my drawings."

The second edition Hirishito picked up and eyed closely, looking at the details. "You are a fine artist son," he said as he thumbed through the pages. "I would like to show you something." Hirishito retreated to his home office, returning a few minutes later with a large black portfolio. Inside were pages of Zen drawings on rice paper. "In my youth, Toshi, I too dreamed of the day when I would be well known for my art."

Toshi held the delicate papers and knew that these must be framed and hung in a place of honor. "I never knew this about you *Chichi*," he said. The feeling of something being missing was still gnawing at him, adding to his growing uneasiness.

"Father," he said in a very low voice. "I have chosen Jayne. I pray that it will not bring dishonor to me or to you, but she is a very rare woman. She understands me. She also loves me for who and what I am. There are no conditions with her, no preconceived notions, no pretense. I come alive when I am in her light. She is ..."

Hirishito touched his son's hand. "Your mother actually likes her a great deal Toshi."

"And you, *Chichi*?"

The silence between them was short as Hirishito smiled at this eldest child. "You have come alive since you have been seeing her. I have never seen you happier. Are you certain that this is not a phase?"

A loud sigh preceded the thoughts which had been troubling him all morning. It is said that when the words are spoken, they take on life. He gave birth to the words. "*Chichi*, I have never wanted to marry, or buy a house to fill it with your grandchildren."

Hirishito's mouth dropped. "*Mago*?"

Toshi burst into laughter. "Not yet, *Chichi*. Not yet, but in the near future. I would like to give you many."

Eri, who had been listening around the corner, burst into the room, asking as well, how they were going to be grandparents since Jayne professed to have no carnal knowledge of Toshi, whose cheeks were now red. Both his parents mouthed, "Oh!" at the same time.

"I would like to ask her to marry me," he said in a hushed voice.

"Are you asking our permission, Toshi? Last night you presented her as if your mind was already made up." Hirishito spoke with his eyes focused on his wife.

"I would like to do so with your blessings and acceptance of her into our family," he said with his head lowered.

Eri wanted to know. "How has her family responded to you?"

"I meet them next week."

"After you speak with them, come back and let us know if you still feel the same way. We will talk more after that, *Musukosan*," Eri told him as she left the room to make herself some lunch. In-laws could often be a deal breaker. From what Eri had seen on some of those reality shows, she wondered if Jayne's *people* were anything close to that.

Toshi sat there, feeling rather dumb. What had been missing and what he could not put his finger on was Jayne's family. She never talked about them. The painting above the couch showed another child, but he had never heard her mention a sibling. Cousins, yes, but a brother or sister, not once. For some reason, that, is what he found unsettling. She had been secretive about her family.

Chapter 26

The whole experience was somewhat surreal. Jayne had never spent the night with a man, let alone took a bath with one. Toshi had introduced her to many firsts last night. The three consecutive orgasms were amazing, but the connection between them was mind boggling. She had never felt so unencumbered and free with her body. The soak in the tub had helped to loosen the sore muscles, but the after effects of his lovemaking covered her like a shroud. She needed to get moving, but if this was what a love hangover felt like, then she was going to become an addict. She definitely wanted a second and third dose.

It was nearly one o'clock when she arrived at The Boll Weevil to meet the girls for lunch. The shroud billowed behind her as she took a seat in the chair and ordered an unsweetened ice tea. Rashunda was the first to notice. "About damned time!"

Jayne only smiled, with a slight blush creeping up her neck, warming her face, but she was not going to bite. Although Toshi had left several marks all over her chest and neck. Jayne turned her head to see where the waitress had gotten off to, when Tamika noticed the very large hickey on her neck.

Tamika, completely overdressed as usual for the casual lunch, asked, "girl, did he make love to you or try to eat you?"

Jayne opened the collar of her blouse and showed them the teeth marks, the hickeys, and a few bruises. "All of the above. I wish one of you had told me how good sex really was....Lord Hammercy!"

The girls broke out in laughter except Brionna, who only made a face. "So you and Mr. Miyagi finally got down to it, huh?"

Jayne was not amused at the reference. "Bri that is a racist comment!"

"Oh so now you have a streak of yellow running up your slit, you want to be all politically correct?" Brionna said with an upturned mouth. Jayne was a bit taken aback by the sudden hostility. She had supported Bri's decisions to date some of the most unsavory characters without any backlash. She wasn't going to allow her friend to believe this was going to be okay with her.

"Have I ever made any disparaging remarks about any man you have dated? Not even when you brought that big ass Grape Ape to meet us," Jayne said as she leaned forward on the table. Rashunda and Tamika both dropped their heads to hide their laughter, especially considering it was the label they both had given to Tyrone.

Tamika played peacemaker. "Jayne, you never did say what Toshi did for a living."

Jayne was all smiles as she told them about his job at the university. It took a concerted effort to not seem boastful as she spoke of how neat his office was in comparison to any professor she had. As well as their work on the comic book. Rashunda reminded her to get everything in writing before they went any further.

"Girl," Jayne said. "You know me better than that. My cousin is a lawyer who drew up all the paper work, filed for our LLC, set up the accounts and everything. So, regardless of what happens, we have the option to buy each other out, or continue on." The waitress had returned with their drinks and took their lunch orders.

Tamika was smiling. "You seem so happy Jayne."

"I am. I really am." She stuck out her tongue. "I felt like Goldilocks last night, ya'll." She started to giggle. "I'll tell you the truth. The first one I had, was way too small and I was a virgin." Her friends chuckled as she went on. "The second was way too big!"

"Ain't no such thing as too big. You need to speak for yourself," Rashunda said as she crossed her legs.

Jayne shook her head. "Oh yes it is! I am a petite woman and I was not about to let that fool ruin my reproductive system and have my pocketbook looking like an over worn turtle neck sweater!"

Tamika asked, "so I guess that means Toshi was just right?"

Jayne was nodding her head up and down like a bobble headed fool. "It was so fantastic, I had to stop him and ask him if it was supposed to feel that good?" Laughter was filling the air, but something was amiss with Brionna.

"Yes, you'd better enjoy it now Jayne. They may sleep with you, but he isn't about to take you home to meet his folks," Brionna added as she twisted in the seat, looking for the waitress.

Jayne watched her face closely as she shared the next bit of information. "I met his parents last night. You will never guess who his father is..." She paused for affect. "Hirishito Yamaguchi! He owns Hirishito's." Rashunda commented how she loved the food there. Tamika was complementary on the sushi bar and wine selections. Brionna seemed to fill up with rage.

"Oh, aren't you the lucky one?"

"Bri, is everything okay with you?" Jayne asked.

"Yes," she said as she snapped at the waitress for being too slow. "I'm just saying, all of a sudden, you go all interracial, when there are good black men out there who work hard to provide for their families. Good black men who are looking for a good black woman."

"They are so hard to find Bri. I know what you are saying and I agree, but this man makes me happy." She looked at each of them. "I love him."

"Yeah, but does he love you back Jayne?" Tamika wanted to know.

The internal smile that she woke up with now radiated through her pores. "He presented me to his parents as the woman he has chosen to share his life with." The waitress returned with their orders. Brionna snapped at the server again. "I expect you to take 10% off the checks for your slowness."

"Calm down Bri. What is going on with you?" Jayne was truly concerned now and wanted to understand what this was all about.

Brionna stabbed a piece of chicken in her salad with the fork. "Ain't a damned thing wrong with me! I am just wondering what the hell is wrong with you! An Asian man, Jayne! Really? You sit here and rub it in our faces that his father is wealthy and he is a professor. Like what our men do isn't good enough!"

For Jayne, this was entirely too much. Especially from a friend that she had supported unconditionally through years of bad relationships. It was one of those rare moments in her life when she truly wanted to curse a bitch out. She was going to, just in her nice nasty way.

"Surely, you must be joking Brionna! After years of parading homeboy after thug in front of us as your next project in the black man renaissance?"

"Black man renaissance, Jayne? Don't make me start cussin'!" Brionna said as she picked up her iced tea, splashing the brown liquid on the table.

"Cuss all you want to, but it isn't going to change shit. Not now, not tomorrow, or next year," Jayne said as she pointed her finger at her. Rashunda and Tamika's eyes got wide. "It is your choice of who shares your life Bri and we have been supportive. Don't get mad at me because my man works behind a lectern and yours behind a garbage truck! You sat with us, talking shit and bragging about him going places on his job and moving up. Hell, he has nowhere else to go but up! If he went down, he would be working at the dump site."

Tamika's eyes were wide and Rashunda put her hand on Jayne's arm, shaking her head at her as if to scold her. "Don't try to scold me like I'm a child Rashunda! The man works in my grandmother's neighborhood and has for the past five years. Everyone in the neighborhood knows him. If you want to scold anyone, you should be scolding her for not being honest. He's going places my ass! He sure is! Around the next corner to pick up a load of someone's trash! We don't judge you! Why the hell are you judging me?"

Brionna reached for her purse to get up and leave, but Jayne was galloping at a full sprint and headed for home plate. "Sit your silly ass down!" Brionna jumped at the harshness of the tone that came from Jayne. "I am your friend and you are mine. You will either tell us what is bothering you or if you walk away, you can forget calling me with your sad ass apology for being such a witch. Now, what is this all about?"

Brionna, now in tears, held her head low. "Tyrone dumped me! He said I was trying to change who he was and that if I couldn't accept him as he is, then he wanted nothing else to do with me."

The circle of trust was reopened as Jayne, Tamika and Rashunda encircled their friend, showering her with consolations. Words of encouragement were issued as the four put their heads together to come up with a plan to help her win back Tyrone.

Chapter 27

Toshi arrived at Farmhaus Burger's on Broad Street to meet the guys for lunch. The turning of his stomach and the unsettled nerves put him in an odd mood, which his friends immediately picked up on.

"I am not sure what is going on with me guys, but I think I need all three of you to go with me to the jewelry store."

Phở wanted to know why and a wide eyed Toshi answered. "I need you guys to make sure that I don't buy everything up in that motherf….."

"Whoa," Raheem said, cutting Toshi off. They were more surprised by his use of language, since he rarely if ever, cursed. "Is it that serious?"

Toshi's head hung low. "The flame burned hot and it burned true. It even burned blue. I am so in trouble. Man, she had to make me move off of her."

Raheem laughed. "Were you squashing her, or just didn't want to let go?"

Toshi, almost ashamed admitted. "No, I just wanted her to hold me."

Laughter went around the table for their friend, who still had not raised his head. "I am thinking about going to the bank on Monday to get a loan."

Felix piped up. "How big of a ring are you planning to buy her, four carats?"

"No and what… make her a target? Have you seen her hands? Jayne is a small woman. What would she do with four carats?" He paused for a brief second to collect his thoughts. "I want to buy her a house with a painting studio," Toshi said softly without barely believing he was uttering the words.

He looked up at his friends. His face riddled with confusion. "What is wrong with me? I feel all funny inside, guys."

Raheem answered somberly. "You, my friend, are in love."

His eyebrows shot up, his forehead crinkled, and his nose snorted contempt for Raheem's words. "Is that what this is? This feeling that has been hovering over me all morning?"

His friends bobbed their heads as if the Dali Lama had just spoken an absolute truth. Felix asked, "You are serious about buying her a house?"

"Yes. I want to fill her and the house with beautiful Blasian babies." He dropped his head again. "Does this feeling ease off any?"

Felix added, "no. It only intensifies especially when you find out your wife is pregnant and you are going to be a father." Everyone at the table looked at Felix who was smiling and handing out cigars from his backpack. The mood was high and festive as the group celebrated Felix's great news. The mood got even brighter as Toshi shared the comic books, showing off the collaboration with his beautiful Jayne.

The light mood was still surrounding him when Jayne arrived at five, to work on the next steps. He greeted her at the door with a light kiss. "How was your day?"

"It was odd, but good," she told him as she made her way to the office.

"Pretty much the same here," he said as he watched her remove a few more copies of the comics from her bag. "I have been thinking about the future."

Jayne turned, without any expression on her face and looked at him. Asking, but not asking.

"Even after the Anime Expo in July, there are other cons, more costumes, and we have a minimum order on the comics, right? So we have to buy at least 5,000 copies of each?"

Still uncertain of where he was going with this. "Yes, not to mention the following editions."

"We need more space Jayne. We need to start looking for a house." He handed her a red marker and took a seat at the desk. "With maybe a second building or a third floor or something."

"Uhmmm, okay," she said, accepting the marker and getting to work.

"I will call an agent on Monday," he told her as he opened the first page of the first edition. "Starting in the upper left quadrant, panel by panel. Let's review."

That was it. Wait. *That was it?* Jayne tried hard to focus, but did he just say he was going to buy a house for them? For the business? For himself? Toshi said nothing more as the next four hours sped by. The review of the comics were complete. Jayne's neck was tight and she felt like she wanted to run away.

"I am really sore and stiff," she told him as she packed up her belongings.

“Start the shower and I will join you in a minute.” His focus was still on the third edition. “I think this cover should be orange, instead of this red.”

She chuckled a bit. “I’m heading home Toshi. Yes, I think a tangerine color would make it pop more.”

“Give me a minute to pack a bag and I’ll be ready to go as well.”

“Toshi, you....” She started but wasn’t sure what to say to him. “I’m not sure....ahhh, I....”

He set down the markers and took both of her hands into his. “Jayne, I don’t care where we sleep as long as I wake up next to you.”

“You do realize you said that out loud right?”

“I know exactly what I said,” he told her as he pulled her into his arms. The kiss was intended to ignite her flame but instead, acted as an accelerant. Jayne felt like a hussy as she pulled him into the bedroom, yanking down his pants while tugging at her own. One leg was still on as she climbed on top of him and guided him inside. She raised and lowered her hips as if she was setting a horse into a canter, pulling at him while setting an even rhythm. He called her name as he ripped open her blouse. His lips and tongue kissing, licking, and suckling at her skin. Toshi didn’t even bother to remove her bra but pushed it above her breasts instead as he took one of the creamy mounds into his mouth. The pace intensified as she came upon her release. “Toshi!” She cried out, throwing her head back, bucking her hips furiously, and howling as if the moon was changing. She found her release, but he flipped her to her back as he began to work on his own.

Gentle words of encouragement were whispered into her ear as he plunged deep inside her. Whispering her name and telling her how good she felt surrounding him. Her hands felt like magic under his shirt as delicate fingers ran over his skin, sinking in. "Oh, Oh, Oh!" She cried out. "I'm ready again Toshi!" This caused him to thrust harder. Each movement had meaning and purpose as he brought them both to climax. They collapsed together in the bed, holding each other in a mass of tangled clothing, sweaty bodies and wrinkled bedding.

"Toshi, you make me feel so good, but this is scaring me a bit. I feel like a wanton woman."

As much as he hated to admit it. "It's scaring me a bit too Jayne." He pulled her into his arms, kissing her on her nose. "I am so in love with you that I am willing to tackle any and every thing that comes our way."

"I think I can live with that," she said with her voice full of laughter.

"But it also means living with me." The words came forth in a soft caress as his hands rubbed at her back.

"One step at a time okay? You have yet to meet my family," she told him as a gentle reminder that they were not ready to set up shop.

"As long as we stand together, I think we will be okay."

Those words were easier said than held. Toshi hadn't met Grandma Pearl or Grandpa Joe. Those two characters could test the patience of Job.

Chapter 28

It was a crazy week, filled with hesitation, trepidation, and knots in her stomach. Saturday afternoon, Toshi was coming to meet her folks. The one thing that kept humming in her mind...*does he love me enough to deal with those two*? Although her body craved his touch, she managed to keep her clothes on the two times in the week she had seen him. By Friday, she was ready to go to his office, lock the door, and mount him on his desk, but she stood firm.

Saturday morning arrived and she was in a tizzy. Toshi made an attempt to hold her until her nerves settled. "No! She will smell you on me, start praying and lock herself in the damned closet!"

"What?" he said in disbelief.

"My grandmother is a bible thumping head case," she said out loud before the flood gate of tears opened.

Toshi held her head as the tears flowed freely. "I never talk about my family because it is just too....." She cried louder, only this time she pulled away and flung herself onto the couch.

"Do you think either of them will ask if I am performing Asian sex tricks on you?" he asked with arched brows.

Jayne looked up at him with a weak smile, but Toshi continued, "Well, isn't that what my mother asked about you? Seriously Jayne, we handle it together. Family is not going to change. We learn to accept each person as they are and for who they are. You love them regardless and continue to live your life. There is nothing more a person can do."

Those words calmed her as she cleaned her face and climbed into the passenger seat of his car. Ready or not, here they come. Toshi was about to meet Grandpa Joe and Grandma Pearl. Jayne stared out the window as she entered her own prayer closet.

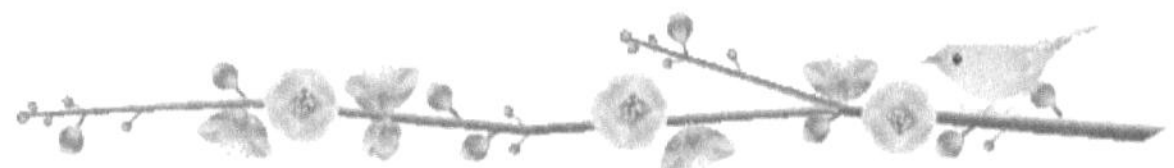

Joseph and Pearlie Carter lived in a four bedroom craftsman style home on a small dead end street off of Walton Way. The yard was immaculate with blooming flowers year round and comfortable rockers which adorned the front porch. Because it was the last house on the dead end street, Joseph had cleared the adjoining lot years ago to cut down on snakes and varmints, but to also make a play area for his four children. Over the years, the cleared lot had served as a baseball diamond, a football field, and an open field for Summer cookouts and parties.

Joseph Jr. was a police officer with three large male children, who were all in law enforcement. Sydney was a computer whiz with two tech savvy children. One who worked for Google and the other for Microsoft. Sydney complained that they never came home often enough. Frank was a civil service employee who had recently retired, with three children. One who was an attorney, the second a crack head, and the third left hitchhiking for parts unknown six years ago and had not been heard from since. The youngest of the brood was Lillie, whom Grandpa Joe always thought was a delicate flower. It befuddled Jayne within an inch of her sanity why everyone chose to show up today.

The street in front of the house was filled with cars and the front porch looked like it does on Thanksgiving Day. It was filled with family. Jayne nearly stopped breathing, but was able to get out the words which truly epitomized how she felt. "Frack, frack, frackety, frack, frack, frackerstein!"

"Jayne, what's wrong?" Toshi asked, now getting really nervous.

She turned in the seat, eyes full of tears. "Let's just keep driving Toshi. We can run away and never look back. We can create our own little private oasis and never have to see any of these people again."

Toshi pulled his Mazda into an empty space and turned the car off. Taking her hands into his. "Are you ready to move with me Jayne?" A weak smile formed through the tears. "Jayne, I need you to move with me. Can we move forward together Jayne?"

Sobs were choked back and she tried to smile. "Fuck you Toshi!" He erupted into laughter.

"Jayne, it is just your family. Either they will like me or hate me, but it will not change how we feel about each other."

"Okay, okay. I can do this," she told him as he wiped away her tears.

"Jayne. Am I the first guy you ever brought to meet your folks?"

"Yes. You are the only person I have ever brought home."

A gigantic grin formed as he started moving with his

hands in the air to some imaginary music in his head. "Toshi what are you doing?"

"You love yourself some Toshi." He started rolling his fist like John Travolta in Saturday Night Fever.

Her eyes rolled upward. "I am having a panic attack, cursing like a sailor and you are celebrating whatever victory you think this is....." Her voice trailed off.

"Jayne, I am celebrating the simple reality that you love me."

"You are right. I do."

He put his hand on the door handle. "Well come on Baby! Let's present the man who won your heart to your family."

"Just like that, Toshi?"

"Exactly like that," he told her as he made his way around the car and opened the door for her. "And later..." He whispered in her ear all the things he planned to do to her later in bed, which made Jayne turn around and reach for the car door. He grabbed her hand pulling her towards the house, and hand in hand they approached the house. Everything had a price and she was ready to pay the cost for happiness with this man.

As they approached the front porch, her Uncles, Sydney and Frank were seated in the rockers, arguing the points between a laptop and a tablet. The argument was stopped only long enough to shake Toshi's hand and pose the question to him, "What do you have, Son?"

Toshi leaned in to the two gentlemen. "I have a two in one combo in a Lenovo Idea Pad, with a 15 inch monitor with a touchscreen. I have the best of both worlds." This answer seemed to please them both, who now decided to argue on the best touchscreen computers.

Jean, Uncle Frank's daughter, exiting the front door with a cup of coffee in her hand greeted them both. "Hey Doc! Hiya Jayne!" She then joined her father on the porch. Jean processed their paperwork to set up their company as well as details of their partnership. She gave her younger cousin a hug and patted Toshi on the shoulder. Uncle Sydney sat up in the rocker. "Did you call him Doc?" This prompted Jean to tell the two men all about Jayne and Toshi's business venture, leaving them room to escape.

In the living room, in front of the flat screen where Grandpa Joe spent many of his days, sat three large men with police haircuts, police officer stares and anger oozing from their pores. Jayne introduced them all to Toshi, who looked up at the six foot tall men that towered over him by several inches. Pride filled her heart as a five foot eight inch Toshi stood his ground, accepting firm hand shakes, making eye contact, and committing each name to memory.

Grandpa Joe and Grandma Pearl were in the kitchen when they entered. Jayne watched as their eyes took him in. He wore black slacks and black shoes with a cream colored shirt with a coordinating tie. "It is a pleasure to meet you sir," Toshi told him as he shook Grandpa Joe's large meaty hand.

He turned to Grandma Pearl who immediately asked, "Jesus is my redeemer, and all praise to the Almighty. What are you Chile? Shinto? Buddhist? Atheist?"

"He is mine as well, Mrs. Carter, and we are

Methodist." That took all the guff out of Pearlie's sails.

"Well, don't that beat all, Pearlie Mae! They are Methodist!" Grandpa Joe added as he slapped his knee.

Grandma Pearl was not to be outdone. "We're getting ready to eat. You two get into that dining room and get the table set."

Toshi seemed unfazed as he followed her around the corner to the formal dining room and nearly tripped over Jayne as she stopped cold in her steps. "Toshi, these are my parents. Malik and Lillie Wright."

Chapter 29

Jayne looked a great deal like her father. She had inherited his light brown eyes and the gap in his teeth. She had her mother's height and build. Toshi shook both of their hands and watched with interest as Jayne failed to embrace either parent, but continued to set the table as if nothing was amiss. Toshi could feel the tension in the room.

"Excuse me while I get some water," Toshi said as he left the room and went back to the kitchen.

Jayne was furious. "Why are you two here now playing the role of loving and concerned parents? As a matter of fact, why are you two here at all?" The words almost came out in a hiss.

"We are still your parents and you will act like you have some sense," Lillie told her in a not too friendly tone.

Malik took a different approach. "Pearlie Mae said you were serious about this young man and I wanted to meet him."

Jayne's face had crinkled up like an old Shar-Pei. "That makes absolutely no sense at all, considering you have never shown up for anything else in my life!"

He took a step forward as Jayne took two steps back. "That is not true Jayne."

"Sending a monthly check is a means of support, but it doesn't have the same connotation and real support, Malik."

"Jayne, you are being way too fresh mouthed with your father. You're not supposed to call either of us by our first names. We are not your pals or friends. We are your parents."

"No, Joseph and Pearlie Mae are my parents! You are two selfish people who have forsaken your responsibilities as parents! You abandoned me!"

A large folder sat in the chair that Malik retrieved. He pulled out a picture of Jayne at her kindergarten graduation and showed it to her. "I don't remember this picture. Where did you get it?"

"I took it, Jayne," he told her as he removed from the folder, photo after photo of her from kindergarten, in soccer and volleyball games, gymnastics events, and even a picture of her at the prom. His eyes were teary. "You looked so beautiful on prom night. I could barely take the pictures. My hands were shaking so badly." Other pictures were of her first car, packing the car for college, and even moving into her apartment. "I tried not to miss anything."

"A bunch of pictures don't mean a damned thing to me, Malik! What, you posing a voyeuristic Father with a camera fetish is supposed to mean something to me?"

Lillie stepped forward and raised her hand as if she were about to strike Jayne, who turned to look at her with so much hate in her eyes, that Lillie stopped cold. "If you lay one finger on me lady, I will put a bullet in you! I will continue pulling the trigger until I unload the clip into that screwed up head of yours!"

Jayne's breathing had become labored as she held her fist to her sides. "We deserve your anger," Malik said with his shoulders slumped, gathering his cache of photos and putting them back in the folder. "I am here, because I failed you as a father. I failed your mother as a husband, but I have worked hard for 27 years to give you everything you wanted and needed. I even picked out your first car Jayne." He wiped at his eyes. "I didn't come back into your life physically because I was afraid I would screw you up too."

Today was not the day to resolve any of these issues. "Why are you here now?"

"I am hoping," Malik said. "As you start this new phase of your life, that I can be a part of it. And maybe when the time comes, be a part of my grandchildren's life."

"Are you saying that I have no brothers and sisters out there, among your many love interests and afternoon humps," Jayne added with venom.

Malik closed the folder, tucking it under his arm. "You are my only child Jayne. You are the one thing that keeps me going each day."

Jayne looked to Lillie who was sitting in the chair with her head down. "And what sorry excuse do you have Lillie?"

Chin stuck in the air, eyes full of resolve, "I have no excuses and I am not going to explain myself you to because until you have lost a child, you have no idea what I went through."

"And you know what Lillie? I don't give a shit. I know you lost a child, but you still had one living that you handed off like a pair of shoes that had started to pinch your feet."

Malik attempted to say something when Jayne held up her hand. "Grandma Pearl raised me in church and taught me forgiveness, but until today, I never realized how angry, bitter, and resentful I was toward the two of you. I don't forgive either of you. In my heart, I know I was better off without you, but it still hurts to be abandoned."

Lillie wiped away tears, but Jayne wasn't finished. "You two can go crawl back into whatever holes you climbed out of, because I don't want or need either of you in my life at this point. And just so we are clear, I never plan to have any children, so if you are resting your hopes in redemption on your grandchildren, then you have come up short again."

She grabbed her purse and went to find Toshi, who was sitting at the table playing Gin Rummy with Grandpa Joe. She touched him on the shoulder. "Toshi, we are leaving."

Grandma Pearl opened her mouth. "God said to turn the other cheek Chile."

"The only cheek I plan to turn to those two are the ones holding up my ass." She turned her back to her grandparents and made her way out the door with Toshi on her heels. "It was nice to meet everyone," he said as he made his way to the car.

Tears rolled down Jayne's cheeks as he drove them home. They arrived at her building and he walked her to the door. "Toshi, I just want to be alone tonight okay."

"No, it is not okay. The last thing you need right now is to be alone."

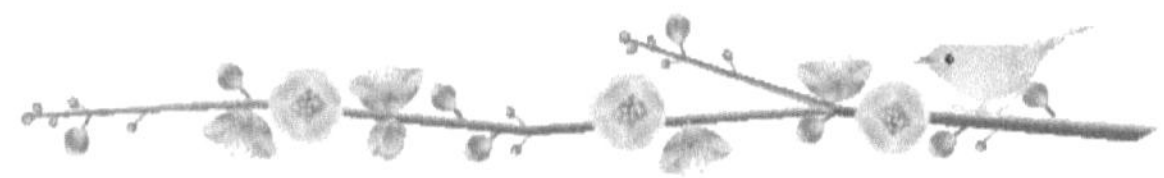

Sunday after church, Toshi sat in his parent's kitchen. Eri was chomping at the bit. "*Musukosan,* did you meet her people?"

"I did *Haha,*" he told his mother, but his eyes were on his father. "They are a learned family in law enforcement. One is an attorney. She has a cousin who works for Microsoft and one who works for Google."

Eri asked, "And her parents?"

In actuality his words were true. "Jayne is truly loved by her family and her parents, who have kept a watchful eye over their only child."

Hirishito asked, "What does this mean for you Toshi?"

"I would like your blessing to make Jayne my wife," he told them both. Kunio sat quietly watching him, feeling proud of her brother for standing up for the woman he loved. She also knew that she would never feel for Akira what her brother felt for Jayne.

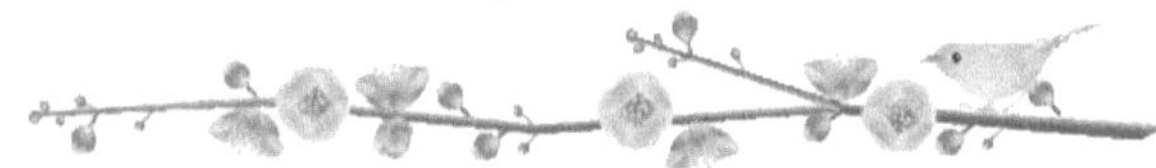

On Sunday after church, Jayne sat on the front porch with Grandpa Joe, with a heavy heart. "Jayne," he said to her as he sipped at his lemonade. "I went to the Piggly Wiggly one time to get Pearlie a watermelon and left Sydney on the cash register. I got half way home before I realized that I left my child."

She looked at him with some amusement. "When I got back to that store, he was balling like a banshee."

He sipped some more lemonade. "Don't smile too big, girlie. I left your little ass a few times as well." He laughed loudly. "There is no handbook on how to be a great parent, because each child is different. What worked on Joe Jr. never worked on Frank and sure as hell didn't work on your Mama. She was that kid on the playground, that if you didn't play her way, then she would take the ball into the house, and nobody could play. We planted them in the same soil, fed and watered them each the same, but your Mama, was different. It was her way or no way."

He rocked back and forth a few times in the chair. "We took her to the doctor several times, telling them something was wrong with that child. They put Pearlie on medication. Giving her a three month supply of some damned Valiums."

He looked resigned in his thoughts. "Failure has a way of showing you what you are made of. Not all of our failures are the ones you can bounce back from. Pearlie took to the prayer closet hoping to pray away the demons she thought riddled Lillie's mind. I am not saying it is our fault, but Lillie was never a strong minded child. She was more like my sister, May Bell, who would change her mind sixteen times to Sunday, before making a decision. But once she made one, she stuck to it. Right, wrong, or indifferent."

Jayne rocked silently in the chair, adding no commentary either way. "They came back for you several times little Jayne, but we would not let you go."

"He stood on this very same porch, yelling at the top of his lungs, that you all were going to be a family again." Grandpa Joe chuffed. "Six months later, they were fighting. He asked for a divorce and she locked herself back in the looney bin for four years. Only reason she left then is because they kicked her sorry butt out."

The look on Jayne's face nearly said it all. Grandpa Joe held up his hand to silence her. "I love my daughter, Chile, but I had to make a choice. I chose to keep you away from those selfish assholes. If you want to be resentful about not knowing your parents, then you aim it at me."

Jayne wrapped her arms around her grandfather's neck. "Girlie, Toshi is a nice young man. Don't hold back on giving him some pretty little Blackanese babies out of fear that you will turn into your parents."

"They are called Blasian, Grandpa," she told him as she let go of his neck. Grandpa Joe reached into his shirt pocket and removed a business card, handing it to Jayne who eyed the card with some trepidation. "When you feel you are ready, give him a call."

As Jayne left the porch, she could hear him mumbling about buying diapers for him and the babies. "Whatever you want to call them chillun', they are going to be funny looking just like you," he shouted at her. She found herself laughing at his grumbling about making extra product in his diaper for Pearlie to clean up.

Chapter 30

The past three weeks had been a whirlwind. June was upon them and the final touches had been made to the comic book which was being printed. The end of the first week of June the books arrived and nearly took over Toshi's home office. Several boxes were taken to Jayne's apartment and everything looked so much smaller. In the midst of all the happenings, Toshi continued looking at houses. When he had narrowed it down to three, he had Jayne join him.

The first house was entirely too large. It was in Columbia County which would make her commute to work miserable. The second house had a lot of potential with a beautiful artist studio with lots of light, but the artist who lived there was not much of a cook. The kitchen was drab, small, and all of the appliances as well as the electrical wiring were outdated. The third house was absolutely perfect, with two out buildings. One to serve as a studio, while the other as a shed for gardening. The only problem, when the door to the studio was opened, what was not drowned out by rattling, they could hear other things slithering. Toshi turned to ask Jayne a question, but she was already back in the car. House hunting had to start over from the beginning.

On Saturday, as Jayne headed to the mall, she became lost in her thoughts. The business card Grandpa Joe had given her held Malik's phone number and work address. Something made her dial the number. After three rings his voice came through the car audio system. "Malik

Wright."

"This is Jayne," she said softly. "It would appear that I inherited my painting ability from you."

His smile was almost audible. "You also inherited that wicked gap in my teeth." They both chuckled while listening to the sound of each other breathing. Jayne asked, "So, how does this work? I mean, where do we start?"

"Let's start here. We build from there, if that is okay with you, Jayne."

"That will work," she responded, pulling over onto a side street.

"Your painting of Mother and Son. I bought it at the gallery showing you had two years ago. It hangs over my dining room table," he told her with pride. "It is so well done and simply beautiful."

The conversation continued on for a few minutes about paints, imagery, and his gallery in Atlanta. It was common ground and safe dialogue, which suited them both fine. The call ended with her promise to come to Atlanta after the LA Expo.

Jayne sat in her car feeling hopeful. Even with so much work to do, she still felt optimistic. *Now, on to the mall….where am I?*

She was sitting on Richmond Avenue, not far from the GRU, Summerville campus in front of an adorable yellow cottage with a for sale sign. She called Toshi. "I found it!" Fifteen minutes later he pulled up in front of the house, which sat on a corner lot. They peered through the window only to be surprised by an older couple, who opened the front door and invited them inside.

The home had beautiful archways, hard wood floors throughout, glazed kitchen cabinets, a double oven in the kitchen, and three bedrooms and three baths. The fireplaces were fantastic, but the selling point for Jayne was the unique custom backsplash in the kitchen. She loved the two fireplaces, but for Toshi, he fell in love with the master bathroom. That had a sunken garden Jacuzzi tub.

The front porch had a swing on it and the patio had a back deck that would be perfect for cookouts and having their friends over. The back yard had a privacy fence and a storage shed. Jayne loved it. "I have to ask. What is the listing price?" she posed to the older couple.

"We are asking $225," they told her. Jayne's heart sank. Even if she paid off her car, that would be a hefty mortgage. Toshi had mentioned buying a house because they needed new workspace, but he hadn't declared her moving in, or making her his wife. At least, thus far he hadn't asked.

Later in the evening, as they sat on her couch, her mind wandered to the little cottage with the pretty yellow walls. In the second bedroom she envisioned a pink wall that she could paint a fairy tale scene upon where a little girl would make it a world of her own. A rocking chair would be in the room where she would sit and nurse their daughter. Her thumb idly rubbed Toshi's hand as pictures flashed before her eyes of a little boy, with jet black hair bounding up and down those stairs, dragging in mud from the back yard. Tears ran down her cheeks. She wiped them away with the back of her hands. *Why am I so frickin' emotional?*

"Why are you crying, Jayne? What's wrong?" Toshi asked with concern.

Never in her life had she envisioned herself being a mother. She never truly wanted any children, but in that house she could see a life, a family, and a future with this man. Always afraid to ask for what she wanted. Always afraid to rock the boat. Never willing to pay the cost to truly get in the game. All of her doubts, fears, and baggage went out the window.

She looked at Toshi, voice shaking with emotion. "I want that house and I want to give you a son and daughter to run back and forth up those stairs. I want to make dinner in that kitchen and make love with you in front of the fireplace. I will empty every account I have, sell my car. Whatever we need to do, Toshi, I will do. I want us to start our life together in that house."

He pulled her into his arms and kissed her deeply. "I will talk to the agent tomorrow."

Chapter 31

The last week of June was filled with last minute details. The hotel room had been booked months ago, the plane tickets were purchased months prior, and boxes of comics were loaded at the UPS store headed to LA. The booth cost was nearly two grand. So far, after expenses they were nearly six thousand in the hole. The cost to play in the big arena was hefty, but much of the cost could be recouped in comic book sales.

Jayne felt defeated yet energized as she reminded Toshi. "We will need to sell at least 12,000 copies to recoup the money we have invested. If we do it right, we will have enough for a sizeable down payment for the house." *If that doesn't work, then I will have to find a street corner and sell some booty.*

"Relax Jayne," he told her as he rubbed her back. "As far as I am concerned, what we have accomplished is more than I ever expected. To have all of this and you at my side, is more than I ever dreamed. The rest will work itself out."

"You are always so calm. I love that about you, Toshi."

"You have a calming effect on me. When I am with you, I don't worry about anything. Besides, I have been led to believe that it was my amazing skills in bed that captured your love," he said with a smile.

"Well, that does help a great deal," she said as she rested her arms around his neck. "In three days we are in the air and *The Vigilantes* makes its public debut."

"So, are you ready to take the big stage with some

heavy hitting Cosplayers?"

"Hell no! I am scared out of my mind," she told him. "But I had this idea after seeing you on the dance floor." She pulled away from him and grabbed her iPod from her bag, scrolled through a few songs, then hit play.

"What if we combined our stage appearance with this music, your martial arts and some well-placed danced moves, with a video as a backdrop. I'm sure we'll make a big splash." She started the music and it was *Bodies*, by Drowning Pool.

Toshi stood transfixed listening. Then he began to move. He made a round house kick, as the words reverberated in the room. He did not miss a beat, as he moved across the living room floor. Suddenly he stopped and went into his Zen room and returned with a set of nunchucks and a sword. "Start it over from the top," he told her as he handed her the nunchucks.

"I am not about to knock myself out with those," she said as she gave them back. "My flexibility comes from years of gymnastics training. I can come up with something cleverer than that." She leaned back into a back bend and started walking backwards.

"Where are your gauntlets?" He asked her. Jayne quickly ran into the room to retrieve them from the office and slipped them onto her forearms. The gauntlets she was very proud of the craftsmanship. They were made out of a lightweight steel, that was easily malleable with heat. She had worked closely with a local fabricator to etch in the designs. She returned with them clasped to her wrist.

"Great! When he starts the count in the song, each

time click the gauntlets together," he told her. "Restart it from the top again, please."

He began to move. As the count began she clapped the gauntlets together. "Great that's it Jayne! Go in slow motion like the Matrix, but make the moves bigger!"

"The backdrop should be a visual of the inner city with shadows of *The Others* and the bad guys we are fighting," she told him as she rolled across the floor and came up in a high side kick, with fist pumps, clicking the gauntlets together.

"Sounds good," he said as he went through a series of flicking kicks. "What we really need to know is can we do these moves in those costumes?"

They both stopped in the middle of the floor, staring at each other. Her boots were heavy and the bodice was tight. "Right!" As they took off into the room to try on the costumes.

The music was cued up and they pretended to enter the stage. Toshi began to move about in the leather jacket. Jayne started stomping in the boots, moving slowly behind him in a mock Matrix slow motion backbend, coming up to clap the gauntlets together. "I'll take the second set of counts with my sword." Jayne moved up to center stage, mixing martial arts and gymnastic moves in slow motion.

"On the third set of counts, we need to do something together," she told him. He stopped with a huge smirk covering his face.

"What?"

"Last night in bed. That move you did. The reverse lift with your legs wrapped around my back."

A gigantic grin covered her face. "Let's do it Baby!"

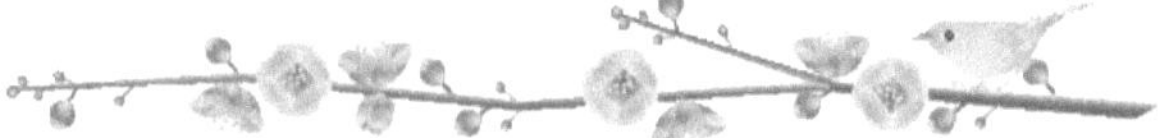

The next day, they needed more space, so they headed to Toshi's parent's house. In the Yamaguchi's backyard, they practiced first without costumes. Eri sat and watched with interest. Twenty minutes later, she was up, giving Jayne pointers, showing her more effeminate martial arts moves.

"Wait, I know what's missing," Eri told them as she darted back into the house. She returned minutes later with small fans that slid perfectly inside of Jayne's gauntlets. "Try using these in the middle portion of the routine."

Hirishito arrived home to hear the loud rock music playing and went to the backyard. Toshi and Jayne were in costume, while Kunio was pretending to be a bad guy sparring with them. And his wife, he wasn't sure *what* she was doing exactly. Everyone stopped when he was spotted.

"Start again from the top," he told them as he sat in the large recliner on the patio. Jayne nodded and Kunio started the music again. At the end of the routine, he stood up with his hands at his sides. "I would like to make a suggestion, if I may." Each listened intently as Hirishito made corrections to some the sword movements Toshi used. He suggested a different approach for Kunio to enter the action and choreographed Jayne's ending scene with a bit more panache.

"Okay, again from the top," he said as he stood back and watched. At the end he said nothing but went back inside the house to retrieve his phone.

"Husband?" Eri asked. "What are you doing?"

"I am buying some tickets to go to L.A. Kunio, are you coming too?"

"Yes, *Chichi*!"

On the first of July, Grandpa Joe and Grandma Pearl drove Jayne to the airport. She introduced them to Toshi's parents, who would be flying out in a few days to join them in Los Angeles. It was sheer luck that Jayne had forgotten to cancel her room reservation, which would serve ideally for the Yamaguchi's, who were now part of the team and set to work in *The Vigilantes* booth. Jayne wasn't worried about the success of the con, since Grandma Pearl had spent the better part of yesterday in the closet praying.

She embraced Toshi in a bosom mushing, nearly suffocating hold. "Take care of our baby, Toshi." After a shake of Grandpa Joe's hand and Jayne's hugging of Eri, they boarded the flight. The costumes had been sent ahead in a separate box from the comics. It was all up to fate from this point forward.

Emotions were running rampant through Jayne as she took her seat by the window of the plane. The warmth of Toshi radiated next to her. Who would have thought ten months ago that this arrogant man would be the perfect guy for her? So much had changed for them both over the past year. The personal growth of sharing a life and a vision for a future together was about to overwhelm her. As she turned to face him, he was staring at her as well.

"I am so in love with you Toshi Yamaguchi. I love you with all my heart." She looked around the cabin to see if the plane had started to crack apart, but nothing was happening.

His fingers intertwined with hers as he reclined his seat. "Good, because I love you too." And with that said, he slept all the way to Los Angeles.

Chapter 32

The flight was ideal as Jayne went over the final pieces of the video show for the Cosplay presentation. Everything was moving along smoothly as they picked up the rental car and drove to the Marriott on West Olympic Boulevard. Although the con did not start for two days, both Jayne and Toshi wanted to check out the lay of the land, pick up supplies, boxes, double check costumes, and prepare for whatever could go wrong.

Toshi had planned for everything to go right. He booked an executive king room with a Jacuzzi tub. He had phoned ahead. Once they checked into the hotel, he suggested they have a light dinner at the Ion Rooftop Patio. It was a clear evening with breathtaking views of the Los Angeles skyline. "Jayne, we are here to have fun."

"There is a cost for everything Toshi. A cost to live, a cost to love, and of course the cost to play with the big boys. We are playing with the big boys here and I am nervous."

"Don't be," he told her as he thanked the waitress for his tea.

"I don't see how you can be so calm about everything," she said with a deep exhalation of air.

"It's easy. We created and produced 3 comic books in less than six months. You launched a website and created an online buzz with a web comic. We have over 1,000 Facebook fans, over 4,000 Twitter followers, and a secret weapon."

Jayne squinted her eyes. “And what is that?”

Toshi leaned forward and took her hand in his. “We have you.”

She only wished she felt the same confidence in her ability as he did. “Tonight, is about me and you Jayne. The rest, we deal with each day. One day at a time. Nothing more, nothing less.”

They finished dinner, toured the hotel to see the features they knew they would not get to enjoy, and headed up to the room. Both understanding, to be at their best, they had to stay in their own time zone and remain hydrated. It may have only been 7 pm in LA, but in Georgia it was 10 o’ clock and moving toward bedtime.

Toshi opened the door to the hotel room and a trail of rose petals led to the bed and bathroom. Jayne’s mouth dropped open as she saw the lit candles and the champagne cooling alongside the chocolate dipped strawberries. Barefoot, they tiptoed across the petals to find the Jacuzzi tub filled with warm water.

“Smooth,” she told him as she unbutton her pants and removed her top.

“I am full of all kinds of surprises,” he told her as he took her into his arms.

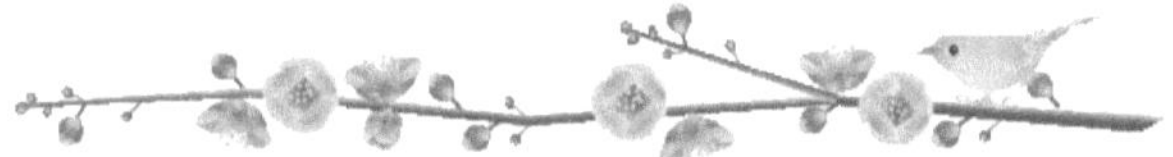

The day before the convention was spent ensuring that tablets were programmed to accept credit cards and that enough change was available for cash sales. Also an extra box arrived.

“What’s in that container Jayne?”

She opened the carton to reveal tee shirts and promo

items that read, *The Vigilantes.* "This is my surprise for you." Toshi donned the tee and stood in the mirror. The cartoon image of himself was on his back, while the front read Katsuo. Jayne pulled out her tee that held an image of her character on the back, with Gauntlet on the front.

"Let's head over to the convention center and check out our space, Katsuo," she said to him.

"Right behind you Gauntlet!"

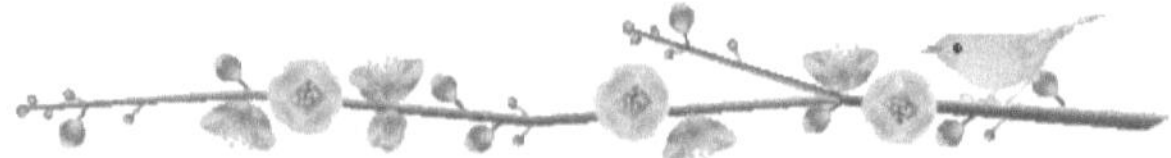

The morning of the con, Jayne checked into the Masquerade at the Cosplay office. Initial judging was taking place this afternoon and she and Toshi had work to do. There were so many exhibitors that her heart sank. There was no way that an unknown comic book with original characters was going to make a splash in the gigantic ocean of products. But they had to try. If they had nothing else going for them, they were loaded with a pocketful of dumb ass hope and three helpings of blind luck. It was all the coins they had left to pay the ferry man. It had to be enough.

In the afternoon, Jayne and Toshi donned their costumes and headed to judging. The marketing professional in Jayne was ready to go as she loaded up her satchel. In the judging room, she and Toshi explained the original designs, patterns, and concept to the judges, whom also received a free copy of the comic along with a complimentary tee and flashlight keychain, which read, *be forever vigilant.* On the way out of the door, she yelled at Toshi, "Katsuo!"

He turned as she clanked her gauntlets together, ran toward him, stepping her right foot into his interlaced hands. Toshi hefted her into the air and she did a back flip to land on the floor in a crouching fighting position.

"Gauntlet!" he yelled. She clanked the cuffs together while he maneuvered through Ninja moves along the floor, coming up behind her, ending in a staged pose in unison, yelling, "Be forever vigilant!"

Everyone in the room begin to clap. Maybe they had a chance after all.

Chapter 33

The Yamaguchi's arrived the morning of the second day of the con. Jayne issued tee shirts to the team, showed them the booth space, and urged them to sell as many as they could. She and Toshi ran to the room to change and took to the show room floor. He as the Silver Samurai and she as Misty Knight.

They returned to the booth in costume to see his parent's eyes grow wide. Kunio loved Jayne's plastic gun and high heeled red boots. "You look so bad ass, Jayne!"

She rolled her neck and gave her a sister girl mouth pout while pulling out her toy gun. "And you know this, Suckas!"

Hirishito broke into laughter. He eyed Toshi's costume details. "Toshi, did you make this?"

"Yes, *Chichi*," he said with his head lowered.

"This is really good work." Hirishito beamed at the details.

"We are heading up to change for the competition which starts in an hour. The booth will need to shut down while you guys go and get ready."

Sales had been sluggish, but Jayne was confident the on stage performance was going to make the difference. An hour later, the five of them stood in the wings. All were nervous. Toshi gathered the team in a small huddle for a pep talk.

"Today, we make history. Today an unknown comic is going to outsell everything in this building. Today, we stand united as a team and as a family. But more importantly, let's have some fun."

All the hands went into the pile, with Jayne doing the count off for the circled up team. Hirishito looked really nervous, but Jayne patted his arm and winked at him. He visibly calmed down. The announcers could be heard over the loud speaker. "Coming to the stage, an original Cosplay design and new to the comic book arena, *The Vigilantes*!"

The music started as Toshi took to the stage with dazzling martial arts moves, plastic nunchucks, and a plastic Samurai sword. The crowd went wild. He was followed on stage by Eri with a fan dance, then Jayne who entered on the count, walking backwards in a backbend. The slide show on the wall behind them displayed aliens landing and bestowing powers upon Gauntlet and Katsuo. The count began in the song as Jayne clinked her gauntlets, moving in slow motion towards Eri, who was followed on stage by Kunio. Toshi's sister was dressed as one of the female assassins from Mortal Combat, which, when she uncovered, his father gave a disapproving look at the scanty outfit.

Jayne moved across the stage to engage with Eri, who began to move with precision with the fans, swinging at Jayne's face. Jayne leaned back into a backbend with slow movements. The second set of counts began as Toshi pulled the Samurai sword and began to move in super slow motion. A ninja suit wearing Hirishito bounded onto the stage moving in tandem with Toshi. As the music segued into the last 30 seconds of their two minute performance, Jayne did a round off, into a backflip on the stage, landing at Toshi's feet. He lifted her, wrapping her legs around his hips, Her body faced the audience as she extracted the fans from her gauntlets and began to mock fight, Hirishito, Kunio, and Eri, who all fell dead to the floor, pretending their throats had been slashed with the fans. Jayne released her legs, rolling into a forward summersault and ending in a crouching position with Toshi standing behind her in a frozen high kick pose. The music stopped and they both yelled into the massive crowd of on lookers. "Be forever vigilant!"

The crowd was on their feet in applause. Toshi helped his parents up from the floor and Jayne locked her arm onto Kunio's as the group took a bow. The primary judged walked over with mic in hand. "That was some performance, right audience?"

The crowd cheered louder. "Tell us about these costumes and The Vigilantes," the announcer asked.

Jayne took the mic. "*The Vigilantes* are original comic book characters and these costumes were made and designed by Dr. Yamaguchi and myself. The comic book is on sale in the lobby at booth J18 from JayTos Comics."

The announcer was amused and sent them off stage to wait for the remaining judging. Several others went after them, but as far as they could see, none of the performances had equaled anything they had presented. Finally, the winners were being announced.

Toshi and Jayne won for best group presentation. Jayne won the award for best intermediate craftsman for the metal gauntlets, which also earned her a new sewing machine. It wasn't the big sewing machine that the master craftsman won, but she was happy. The third place winner went to a woman with big foam formed snakes coming from her insides.

"Second place goes to these new comers, who came in and tried to steal the show!"

Jayne and Toshi waited back staged with baited breath. "*The Vigilantes*! Dr. Toshi Yamaguchi and Jayne Wright!"

Excitement filled her soul as they took to the stage. The announcer asked a few questions. Jayne was so full, she could barely answer. Toshi took the mic. "I just want to say thank you to all of you, my parents and sister who did an awesome job as the assassins. I especially want to say thank you to my right hand, my partner, and the love of my life Jayne Wright."

Shock wasn't the right word she needed to express what she was hearing, but it paled in comparison as Toshi took to a knee. "I think now is the perfect time to ask you, in front of all of these anime fans. Jayne LaQueeda Wright. Will you be my partner in crime fighting and be ever vigilant in the care of my heart and consent to be my wife?"

Tears filled her eyes as he opened the velvet box to remove the daintiest engagement ring that fit her small hand perfectly. "Yes! Yes I will, Toshi!" The crowd roared as they left the stage with check in hand to be congratulated by his parents and sister. Hirishito looked at the check. "That's it? That's a lot of work for $2,000! It cost me more to fly us out here!" Eri pinched him and several of the male characters back stage were flanking Kunio. Toshi stepped in between her and the men, wielding his sword at several who had lust in their eyes. "She is my sister, back off!" Jayne was smiling at him as she linked her arm into Kunio's bringing her closer to the parents. Toshi answered his father.

"*Chichi*, it is the honor and recognition which is important." Toshi told his father, as he pulled his sister away from some suspicious looking men.

His parents and sister headed toward the booth to reopen sales as the two made their way to the photo stands for press ops. They were stopped by many new fans who had tons of questions, but were directed to their booth.

One large framed gentleman stopped them and handed Toshi a business card. "We want to talk to you about possibly making *The Vigilantes*, Agents of S.H.I.E.L.D. Call us next week. Let's open a line of communication." Jayne looked at the card and it said Marvel Comics. This evening could not get any better.

With the photo sessions over, the two headed back to their booth to find a line around the corner. Hirishito and Kunio were running both tablets for credit card sales and Eri was working the middle with cash sales. Jayne and Toshi rounded the corner and were bombarded with people who wanted them to autograph the comic books.

Toshi looked at her, nodding his head. "Secret weapon."

Jayne clicked together her gauntlets. "Let's do it!"

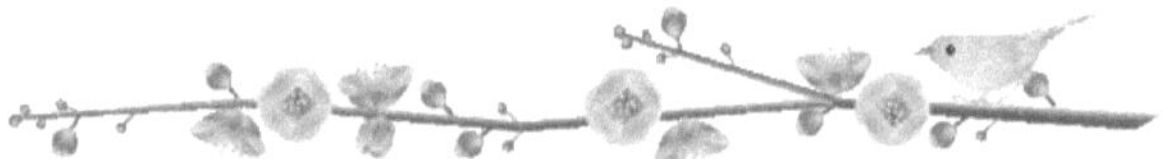

At the end of a very long and weary day, Jayne, freshly showered, in stocking feet climbed upon the king sized bed and sat in the center with her iPad. It was difficult to wrap her mind around so much that had occurred in one day. If the calculations were correct, and another 5,000 copies were sold, then the comic would be seriously in the black as well as have a nice down payment on the house.

Toshi came back to the room to be met with a very serious faced Jayne. "What is that look about?"

"Just doing some math, running prelim numbers, seeing where we need to make some adjustments. If we sell at least 5 to 7,000 more copies in the next two days, we will be set."

He responded by grabbing her by the foot and pulling her toward him. Her bottom teetering on the edge of the mattress. "Jayne, we introduced a new comic book and performed on stage in front of thousands of people, with my parents no less." He continued to talk as he removed her socks. "We won second place for best in show."

Capable fingers unzipped her faux leather pants, tugging the breeches down over her hips. "You won an honorable mention for costume craftsmanship and we sold 6,000 comic books today." The pants were thrown aside as he added, "You also consented to be my wife."

"I know, I know but..." she tried to say as he began to remove his pants. She had the oddest realization. "Toshi, is every pair of underwear you have black?"

"Yep, socks too. It makes doing laundry so much easier," he told her as he pulled her underwear down and over her knees, but knotting them at her ankles to restrict her movement.

"Uhmm, what are you doing?" Jayne asked as she tried to move her legs.

"Some things, you have to appreciate for what they are, others for what they will become. You and I, have created something in six months that most people will never do in 6 years." He spoke softly as he locked her ankles behind his neck, lowering his face.

"Whoa, Toshi, I......"

Her words were lost as his mouth expertly brought her pleasure. "I guess we will discuss the rest..." she attempted to say, but his mouth was driving her insane. "Good gobstoppers!" she cried out as his fingers plunged deep into her recess changing her focus to what he was doing. Nothing else mattered right now, but what they were feeling. Together, they were magical.

Chapter 34

The last two days of the con went far better than either Toshi or Jayne had imagined. Several comic book stores placed orders for the first three editions. Katsuo and Gauntlet were invited to perform at ComicCon. S organizers of South by Southwest handed them a personal invitation to come out in March. On the last day, as they packed up to ship he remaining comic books and costumes home, a collector stopped by their booth and purchased 100 copies of each edition.

The only way the entire experience got any better was when one of the big wigs at DC Comics handed Jayne a business card. "Call me next week," he told her and she handed him one of their cards as well.

"Professional, I like that," he said as he walked away.

Jayne was bone tired and ready to head home. She made a quick call to her grandparents to let them know she and Toshi were headed back to Georgia and he would be giving her a ride home. Even as she settled into the seat on the plane, she made the final calculations on her iPad, turning it to face him, displaying the spreadsheet with the preliminary data.

"Simply amazing," he said as he stared into her eyes. Toshi already knew the numbers as he calculated them in his head 30 minutes before she even started the spreadsheet.

Even after he had fallen asleep, his fingers intertwined into hers. It took Jayne a minute to realize Toshi had been referring to her, not the sales and projections. A slow smile crept across her face as she flipped their hands over and she looked at her engagement ring. It was perfect. Three stones, with a ruby in the center, flanked by two diamonds. It was a nice touch to make her birthstone the focal point of the ring. On her small hand, the stones were complimentary, much like her new fiancé. When he slept, he would either intertwine their legs, fingers or arms, often waking in the same position.

The entire experience had been surreal to Jayne. Never before had she spent the *whole* night with a man. Waking up next to Toshi was amazing. The same man that she had dismissed on more than one occasion for being an insensitive ass, she was going to marry! She watched him sleep, imagining him playing with their son or daughter.

Jayne had never wanted kids, nor had she imagined any in her future. Her parents had been such head cases and her grandmother a religious zealot, making her fearful to even want to try and attempt mothering anyone. She had never brought anyone home before Toshi, either. Not even girlfriends. He was so different, yet they were so much alike. As the plane touched down and he stretched himself awake, he found Jayne staring at him. “Simply amazing,” she told him with a gentle squeeze to his fingers.

His car had been brought to the airport by Phở. As they rolled their luggage out to the parking garage, Toshi was quieter than normal.

“Is something bothering you, Toshi?”

He loaded the luggage in the back and walked around the car to open the passenger door. “No, I am just trying to process how blessed I am to have you, Jayne."

"You do realize you said that out loud right?" She laughed as her arms came up around his neck.

"I love you," he told her as he lowered his head to kiss her deeply. "Let's go home."

On the drive, Jayne fumbled with the iPod, but instead, ended up playing what was in his CD player, which was still the Barry White song. She laughed, but soon noticed he wasn't taking I-520. *Maybe he is going a back route, but there isn't a lot of traffic.*

As the Mazda made its way up Central Avenue, Jayne began to wonder. It was still early and maybe Toshi was stopping by her grandparents so they could see her face. Instead he turned up a side street, then made a left, a right, and pulled into the driveway of the pretty yellow cottage.

Jayne squealed! "Are we going to make them an offer?" She bounded out of the car before he even placed the car in park. She knocked at the door, peered into the window, and then rapped on the glass. "Toshi, I don't think anyone is here." Her nose crinkled with disappointment covering her face, looking as if she had just dropped her ice cream cone.

He walked up slowly, jangling his keys. She still had not paid him any attention until he slipped the key into lock and turned the handle. "How did you get keys to these people's house?" His eyes were wide as she tried to get into the door, but he held up his hand to slow her pace.

He bent down as if to retrieve something and hefted her into his arms, carrying her across the threshold.

"Welcome home, baby." He flicked on the light switch. Her painting hung above the fireplace. The couch was there in the living room and her coffee table. She begin to wiggle to get out of his arms, hitting the floor as she took off up the stairs. He locked the door behind them as he followed her up the stairwell.

In the master bedroom she was relieved that her bed was in there versus the block of hard foam he slept upon. All of their things were here. Her clothes, dressers, and even the items under her sink! She ran into the master bath and sure enough, there those things were!

"How, Toshi..., I don't understand," she said through tears which were threatening to consume her.

"Easy. I was prequalified for the loan and for a quick close, I talked the owners down by two grand. Your dad bought down some points and we sealed it up in 15 days. Our friends moved us in while were gone."

Jayne plopped down on the bed. "Dear Lord!" Her hands flew to her cheeks.

"What's wrong?"

"My grandmother will probably die in that closet on her knees in prayer if she knew you are I were living together and we are not married!"

Toshi was in the bathroom starting the water in the tub, adding bubble bath and soaking salts, while removing his pants. It then registered in her head what he had said. *Your dad bought down some of the points.*

"You said Grandpa Joe bought down some of the points?"

Toshi was already in his underwear, eyeing the tub like a lover welcoming him home. "No, your dad, Malik.

He called and asked what he could do to help. I told him." He peered around the corner, using his finger to beckon her forward. "He also sent that painting in the dining room."

Jayne took off down the stairs to the dining room and turned on the lights. Over the fireplace was a wonderful portrait of a biracial family. With her, Toshi and two small faceless children. The family was enjoying a picnic by the lake. The little boy held a comic book. Jayne moved closer to the painting. The cover read, "The Vigilantes."

"Said it was his wedding present to us." Toshi's voice startled her. His arms encircled her waist, planting a small kiss on her neck and he guided her back up the stairs.

"You are so calm about all of this," she told him as she tested the temperature of the water.

"All I know is..." he told her as he helped her disrobe. "I want to end my evening with you in this tub, and start my day in your arms in that bed." He stepped into the tub, water pooling around his ankles.

She joined him in the water, still frocked with worry. "My dad may be okay with this, but Grammy Pearl is going to anoint your head with oil."

"Jayne." He helped her get comfortable in the large tub. "You'd better plan the wedding fast."

"Oh that is even worse! She is going to think I'm pregnant," she said with some disgust.

"I can make that happen to, if you like," he said with a sheepish grin as he leaned back into the warm water, pulling Jayne against him.

"Not this soon, I hope." She laughed as she allowed the sponge to fill with water.

"Whenever, you are ready, Gauntlet."

Jayne pretended to click her wrist cuffs together like she had on the stage. "We need more time to play Katsuo."

The button was pressed and the jets kicked on, massaging their sore, tired bodies. But something else had been bugging Jayne. "Toshi, I have been meaning to ask you something that has been troubling me a bit and I didn't know how to ask you about it."

"Hmmm?" He mumbled through half closed eyes.

"Why did you have a strip of missing pubic hair?"

.

ABOUT THE AUTHOR

Olivia is an author, a blogger and an adult educator. She writes fiction under the penname of a private hero, her mother, Olivia Gaines Aaron. She holds a Bachelor of Arts in Mass Communication from the University of Alabama at Birmingham and a Master's in Organizational Management.

Olivia Gaines has authored the short story series The Bounty (2009), Vengeance (2012) and The Bounty Hunter (2013). The Slice of Life Series is new in the Olivia Gaines portfolio which includes, Two Nights in Vegas, The Perfect Man, The Basement of Mr. McGee and Letter to My Mother.

In 2011, she completed work on her second novel, Courting Guinevere and has recently completed Loving Words, her 3rd novel, the second book in the Davonshire Series, which will released later in 2014.

www.ingramcontent.com/pod-product-compliance
Lightning Source LLC
Chambersburg PA
CBHW020104180626
46812CB00006B/2467

9780615948157